Ms. Zephyr's Notebook

Also by kc dyer:

The Eagle Glen Trilogy
Seeds of Time (2002)
Secret of Light (2003)
Shades of Red (2005)

Ms. Zephyr's Notebook

by kc dyer

A BOARDWALK BOOK
A MEMBER OF THE DUNDURN GROUP
TORONTO

Editor: Barry Jowett
Designer: Erin Mallory
Proofreader: Marja Appleford
Printer: Webcom

Library and Archives Canada Cataloguing in Publication

Dyer, K. C.
      Ms. Zephyr's notebook / kc dyer.

ISBN 978-1-55002-691-7

      I. Title.

PS8557.Y48M58 2007   jC813'.6   C2007-900860-7

1   2   3   4   5   11   10   09   08   07

Conseil des Arts   **Canada Council**   Canada   ONTARIO ARTS COUNCIL
du Canada   **for the Arts**   CONSEIL DES ARTS DE L'ONTARIO

We acknowledge the support of the **Canada Council for the Arts** and the **Ontario Arts Council** for our publishing program. We also acknowledge the financial support of the **Government of Canada** through the **Book Publishing Industry Development Program** and **The Association for the Export of Canadian Books**, and the **Government of Ontario** through the **Ontario Book Publishers Tax Credit program** and the **Ontario Media Development Corporation**.

Printed and bound in Canada
Printer on recycled paper

www.dundurn.com

Dundurn Press
3 Church Street, Suite 500
Toronto, Ontario, Canada
M5E 1M2

Gazelle Book Services Limited
White Cross Mills
High Town, Lancaster, England
LA1 4XS

Dundurn Press
2250 Military Road
Tonawanda, NY
U.S.A. 14150

Ms. Zephyr's Notebook

For M & P
My reason for everything

1

Night never came here. The lights never dimmed and true stillness never really settled. *No such thing as rest in peace*, Logan thought grimly as he slipped in through the lower entrance door and passed the morgue. In here, even the dead were not given a respectful darkness. Maybe the light was to fool them into thinking they hadn't started their last, long journey. Logan didn't think so. But he didn't have time to ponder the question right now. He had a journey of his own to make.

The one positive about spending so much time in this place was that he knew his way around. Every closet, every cupboard. All the places where he'd be spotted immediately. And all the places he wouldn't. At the end of the basement hallway, the door to the supply closet was slightly ajar. Logan slipped through the opening and the door clicked quietly closed behind him. This closet was perfect. Not often used, out of the way, and most important, unlocked. Nothing special in there. Nothing restricted. Not even doctor's scrubs, which tended to walk out the door if they weren't locked up. Just gowns and flat sheets and big cardboard boxes of toilet paper.

Inside the closet, Logan pulled off his gloves and

jammed them into the pocket of his coat. He crushed the coat flat deep inside the nearest pile of sheets. Checked his boots. It was safe to leave them on, but only if they were dry. The staff around here would spot a trail of water on the floor as quick as thinking.

Under his coat, Logan wore a set of green scrubs, acquired before the nurses began locking some of the supply closets. He'd worn them a lot when he was living here and they were pretty threadbare, but that was the idea. He wanted to look like he fit in. The truly sickening part, the part that made his stomach churn, was that he did fit in. Too well. He'd been here before and he would be here again. But not tonight. Tonight he wasn't here to stay, just to make a brief withdrawal and then be on his way. *Miles to go before I sleep*, he thought.

The route up the back stairs was easy. Almost no one used stairs in a hospital, and certainly never at night. The third-floor stairwell was one of the places he had gone in the past when he needed to escape. And that's where he stood right now, panting only a little. His conditioning was not what it once had been, but it was coming back. A good thing, because speed was his only hope. Speed, and a little luck.

The door handle snapped downward and Logan's heart shot into his throat. By instinct he grabbed the opening door. One of the night cleaners tottered through the gap with her bucket, stumbling a little since her passage had cleared so unexpectedly. Logan caught a glimpse of a sprig of holly tucked into her hairnet before he pulled his face back into the shadow of the door.

"Sorry about that," he mumbled, keeping his head down.

"Oh no, it's all right," she answered, her accent heavy in the dead air of the stairwell. "It is easier to roll my bucket when someone holds the door. Thank you, sir." She pulled her dripping mop from the bucket, cranked a handle to wring out the grey stringy mass, and began to mop the floor at the top of the stairs.

Sir. Logan nodded, his head still turned so she couldn't see his quick grin. Not too many people around this place called him "sir." Couldn't remember it ever happening before, truth be told.

His grin evaporated as he stepped out onto the third floor, pulling the door closed behind him. Only two wards on this floor — Children's and ICU — and things suddenly became a lot stickier. His face might be vaguely recognized around the rest of the hospital, but there he had a certain anonymity shared by all the patients. Here he was a known quantity.

His single advantage was stealth. This was the one place on the planet no one would expect to find him, so if he kept out of the way all should be well. But the next part was the most tricky and he focused his attention on his goal. Deep breath. Move.

The hallway lights had been dimmed to the usual

night-time gloom, but he could still make out two late-shift nurses, busy in the station at the far end of the hall. Logan glanced at his watch. Eleven p.m. As planned, his timing was perfect. The nurses would be assembling pills in tiny paper cups to distribute to the patients during the six o'clock morning parade. His mouth took on a bitter taste and he leaned against the wall for a moment. The thought of years ahead — a whole lifetime of pills in the morning — made a wave of weakness wash over him.

Suddenly, a third nurse stepped out of the room nearest to him and shut the door quietly behind her. Logan ducked back into the shadows. She headed down toward the station and he closed his eyes with relief. If he hadn't paused, he would have arrived at the door just in time to walk right into her face. All his work would have been for nothing.

He could see from her brisk walk that it was Nurse Takehiko. Cleo called her Medusa. Or Cyclops ... or something like that. Logan couldn't really remember; Cleo had weird nicknames for each of the nurses. One time she had told Logan that they were all the names of mythical monsters, but he still couldn't keep them straight. Logan didn't feel Takehiko was so bad, actually. All the same, he didn't want to run into her — or anyone — right now.

There are times when long legs are an asset and this was one of them. Logan peeled a strip of duct tape from his pant leg and crossed the hall in three lanky strides. As he opened the door he slipped the tape over the latch so the door slid silently into place behind him.

The room was in darkness, apart from the blinking LED lamps of the equipment that buzzed and hummed along one wall. The darkness was an asset here, as Logan knew this room more intimately than any other in the hospital. There was space for only a single patient, and it was here he'd spent some of the worst days of his life. It was a place he'd vowed never to come back to. Not for the first time that evening, he thought about turning on his heel and bolting. The smell of the place made him sick. But if he left now, he might as well just go home. And he almost had what he needed — just a few moments more and he could leave. He took a deep breath and waited until his eyes adjusted to the dim light.

The other half of the room had been emptied of its patient furnishings years before. Instead, a tiny, cluttered desk was crammed into one corner of the room. For some reason Logan didn't understand or care about, cutbacks meant that space was at a premium. So this room was shared — by a patient, and during the day, a teacher. Still, thinking back, Logan knew there were worse roommates he could have been stuck with.

Abigail Zephyr had been the in-hospital teacher for extended-term patients since long before Logan had moved in. And Abbie's desk was where he was headed now. She had something he needed — enough to bring him back here to the one place on earth he never wanted to see again. He stepped easily though the dark interior of the room, curtained off from the bed, but not locked. Never locked, because she wanted the kids to be able to find her — or whatever else they needed — at all times.

Logan stepped up to the desk. This side of the room had no beeping or sighing equipment. No window, beyond the glass wall that separated it from the hall outside, and that was heavily curtained to allow the patient what darkness there was to be had. But Logan didn't need light. What he needed was under his hand — and then in his hand. He had the notebook. Time to go.

When the glow came from the bed on the other side of the room it was sudden enough, and bright enough, to make Logan gasp aloud. His eyes had adjusted to the darkness, so the face illuminated in the light from the open computer screen looked brilliant, so white as to be almost blue in the glare. The only other thing Logan could see was a single, pale hand holding a red button on a cord.

"So what's it going to be, Logan? Are you going to tell me why you've got Abbie's notebook, or am I going to call the nurse? Your choice."

2

Logan spoke slowly, trying to keep it casual. "Oh, hi Kip. Sorry, buddy, I didn't mean to wake you."

"You didn't," said Kip. His eyes still looked huge in the light from the computer screen. "I had a game going on my computer when the nurse came in to tell me to go to sleep. I was going to wait five minutes and then start it up again, but you came in first."

Good. He could work with that. "Cool. Which game?"

"Logan, who cares? What the heck are you doing in here? It really scared me when I heard someone sneak in while the lights were off."

Logan's mind whirled. There was no time for talking to Kip — the kid was supposed to be asleep. He had work to do and the last thing he needed was to have to include this kid in his plans. It was going to mess up everything. But Kip held all the cards right now. The power was in his hands — literally.

"Geez, I'm sorry I scared you, dude. I just forgot something when I left last week and this seemed like a good time to come and pick it up. This used to be my room, remember?"

Kip rolled his eyes. "Oh, right. That makes a lot

of sense. Yes, I remember that this used to be your room. I also remember what you said last time you were here. You said if you came back to this hospital, they'd be carrying you on a slab, because you weren't ever going to walk in here on your own two legs again. And so now you break into Abbie's office in the middle of the night and I'm supposed to believe you forgot something?"

Logan chewed on his lower lip. This kid was pretty smart for his age. But he'd set down the call button, and Logan was almost sure the kid wouldn't turn him in. Almost. He shot a sideways glance at the clock on the wall. Every minute he spent here slowed him down. But if the kid gave him away, he'd be far worse off.

Logan stepped closer to Kip's bed. "Did I ever tell you the story about how I got here the first time?"

Kip still looked sceptical, but his eyes softened a little. "No."

Logan tossed the notebook casually on the bottom of the bed. "Mind if I join you?"

Kip grinned and pulled his legs in to his chest. Logan made it a policy to never sit on anyone's bed. He hated the freaking hospital beds. But Kip was just a kid. And if Kip thought they were just hanging out, maybe things could work out the way they were meant to. Maybe.

So Logan hopped up on the bottom of the bed, reached over, and yanked up one of the side bars to lean on. He had a moment's fear as the thing clanged into place, but both he and Kip sat very still and no nurse's feet approached, so all was well. Kip pulled up the blanket and gave a sleepy grin. He was ready to hear a story.

"I hated this place when I came here," Logan said, and Kip nodded his understanding. Anyone who had stayed here would understand. It wasn't the hospital itself, or the people who worked here, or even the stinking smell of the place. Sickness and pain were in these walls. No amount of ammonia could ever scrub that away, and any kid who had to live here awhile knew all about it.

Logan reached over and pulled the notebook into his lap. He'd never told a story to a kid before, and he had to make this one good.

"I don't remember a lot about that first day. I didn't know who Abbie was or what she wanted. All I knew was that I needed to get out of here, and fast."

He opened the cover of the notebook and a flimsy piece of paper fluttered onto his lap. The tape that had stuck the page onto the cover of the notebook adhered to his fingers. He peeled the tape off and smoothed the e-mail back into place.

"What's that?" asked Kip.

Logan shrugged and glanced again at the page.

To: Abbie Zephyr <<u>a_zephyr@evergreen.org</u>>
From: Tom Dangerman <<u>t.dangerman@esd.com</u>>
Re: Your Request

Dear Ms. Zephyr,

I have given your somewhat unusual request a great deal of consideration over the past few days. As you know, it is district policy to ensure all student progress remains entirely private. However, after viewing your arguments and taking into consideration the unique teaching environment at Evergreen Hospital, I have decided to waive the standard practice, providing that student grades continue to be submitted electronically. Your students may submit their work to you in a centralized file folder or notebook as you see fit, providing the grades and comments are available only to the individual student and their parent and/or guardian.

Tom Dangerman
District Administrator,
Evergreen School District 36

Logan began to turn the page, but the tape from the e-mail caught his fingers again and the flimsy paper tore in half. He swore under his breath and ripped the rest of the page out of the notebook.

"It's just some piece of school-board junk. No one will notice it's gone. It's not like anyone reads that crap, anyway."

He tossed the crumpled wad under Kip's bed and flipped through the pages of the notebook. "Here it is," he said softly. "My first day."

November 1
Logan K.   *<parenteral fluids—slow drip IV>*
<u>After breakfast sometime, if I was eating, which I'm not.</u>

Life sucks and then you die.

L.K.

November 1
Logan K.   *<IV fluids, corticosteroids>*
<u>Some time after noon.</u>

Apparently truth is not acceptable, at least not around this place. Here everything has to look clean and smell clean, and bad language is not tolerated. Man, I could really come up with some bad language if I felt like it right now, but I don't. So just forget it.

L.K.

November 1
Logan K.   *<IV fluids, corticosteroids>*
(Bag empty but no one has noticed yet. L.K.)
<u>Ten minutes later.</u>

Okay, Abbie, I give up. You win. Hope you're happy. I'm writing the stupid paragraph, but only so I can get my Xbox back, understand? The days around this place are so <u>totally</u> long and boring that I'll do anything to get back to my gaming. And you get the journal entry that you've been bugging me for. This isn't even real school — I can't believe you expect me to do school work if I'm in the freakin' hospital.

I don't even know why I'm here. I thought the worst thing about today would be a Halloween-party hangover. I don't get this. I'm gonna be out of here by the weekend.

And hey, I've noticed that *I'm* supposed to have ethical standards and not use bad language and all, but for some reason this doesn't apply to everyone else. Like you, for example, Teach. Swearing is out but bribery is allowed? Well, whatever you say, because know what?

18

You've got your paragraph, and then some. And if you want to know how I'm feeling, well, just read between the lines, okay? Because I'm done.

L.K

November 4
Logan K.　　*<IV fluids, corticosteroids>*

(10th bag in 3 days, Abs. All I do is pee. L.K.)

<u>Morning, I guess.</u>

Geez, you'd think if a person is sick enough to be in the hospital they wouldn't have to do school work. This is going to be one cheerful journal, Abbie. I hope you enjoy it. Here's the information you're after, not that you really care or anything. Let's see ... Logan Kemp, age 15. Loves: Rugby, cars, computer gaming. Hates: School, this place, and most of all, my own guts. Yeah — pretty freakin' cheerful. Always looking on the bright side, that's me.

You find a bright side for me to look at and I will, Abbie. I'm supposed to be at rugby practice after school today. Instead, I'm stuck in here for who knows how long. My gut is killing me and nobody can tell me why.

You told me to write about something that interests me. You know what? Nothing interests me. Not in here, anyway. This place stinks. And I mean that literally. It stinks of Lysol or chlorine or some other kind of solvent that they use to clean up after dead people and disgusting living people who vomit all over themselves and the floor. Or those real losers who shit their pants.

Sorry, Abbie, but that one was worth it. So take my game away for an extra hour. It's not going to change the fact that one of those losers is me.

Logan.

Evergreen Hospital
Dining and Catering
Department

To: Takehiko Ken, RN, Children's Ward
cc. Ms. Abigail Zephyr,
   Evergreen Hospital Education Department Head

Re: Patient Dietary Requirements

This is to confirm that meal and menu planning has been suspended for patient Logan Kemp, who has been placed by Dr. Valens on total parenteral nutrition, administered intravenously.

Thank you.
Alma Bellona, Hospital Dietician

November 5

Logan K.   *<IV drip, analgesic, antiemetic>*

Morning, at some point.

Okay, Abbie, I'm doing my thing, just like a good boy. Here's your journal entry, since I can actually think of something to write. Because today there was a bit of excitement around this stupid hick-town hospital. You must love it, Abbie, 'cause it looks like you've landed yourself another victim.

So here's the scoop. Sometime yesterday afternoon I hauled this Useless Contraption attached to my arm downstairs to the hole in the wall they call a "gift shop." All I needed was a pair of decent batteries — no hope, of course. Now, if I'd wanted a hand-knitted toilet paper cover, it would have rocked. They had at least five of those.

I was just dragging Useless back to the elevator when the ambulance entrance doors flew open and the boys came flying in, pushing what looked like some bag lady on their cart.

Those poor guys. You've really got to feel for them. I mean, they get the excitement of racing through red lights and blaring the siren and all, but once they dump the contents of the stretcher into Emerg, well, they're stuck here like gum to a shoe until whoever they've scraped off the highway is actually admitted.

But their lost freedom was my gained information. The nurses hauled Bag Lady onto a hospital gurney and whipped her out of sight. Good thing, too. She stunk like she'd peed herself. One of the ambulance guys slumped down into a chair and the other one went trolling for junk in the machines along the wall. I scammed a choc— ah, well, never mind what I scammed from him, Abbie. Let's just say it wasn't on my list of prescribed dining.

So I hauled Useless over ...

Aw, geez. Looks like the vampires are back for more of my blood. Later, skater.

L.K.

WHILE YOU WERE OUT

Abbie Z,

Dr. Valens has been trying to reach you regarding a new patient. Pls page him at #516

Thx
Karna, Reception

Evergreen High School
Interim Report

Date: November 5
Subject: English 10
Teacher: Mr. Jose Diego
Student Name: Logan Kemp
Student Number: 010461
Reason for Report: Student transfer
Current Class Standing: 63% [C]

Details:

This mid-term report is being produced at the request of Ms. Angela Kemp as a result of her son's short-term transfer from our school to the Evergreen Hospital facility.

This is my second year as Logan's English teacher. Logan seems to be working at a slightly lower productivity level than last year. Perhaps this can be attributed to his illness. As can be seen from his current grade standing, his effort in the class is only marginally above average. Logan does fairly well on in-class tests, however 6 of the 10 homework assignments expected so far this year have not yet been submitted.

I was very sorry to hear of the sudden onset of Logan's illness and hope he is back at school soon. Perhaps his time in the hospital can best be used by making up some of his missing assignments.

Respectfully submitted,
Jose Diego
Evergreen High School
English Department Head

cc. **Mr. Harold Duke,**
   Principal, Evergreen High
   Mr. Jake Arnold,
   Athletic Department Head, Evergreen High
   Ms. Abbie Zephyr,
   Teacher, Evergreen Hospital
   Mr. Carter Kemp & Mrs. Angela Kemp,
   parents

November 5
Logan K.   *<IV—Total Parenteral Nutrition, TPN>*
<u>Around sunset, maybe? Can't really tell.</u>

Those nurses really know how to screw up a story. Okay, where was I? Oh yeah ... so I moseyed on over to the chairs and plopped myself down between the attendants.

"Nice bag lady," I said to the air.

The dude eating the chocolate gave me the eye. You know the look, Abbie, 'cause you do it so well. The old better-be-nice-to-the-kid-maybe-he's-dying look.

"She's no bag lady," he said, kind of cautious.

The other guy leaned back in his chair and reached behind me to poke the first dude, warning-like.

"What? I was just making a comment. No need to poke your buddy there ..." I leaned forward and read his name badge, "... uh, Shawn."

"Listen, kid." Shawn's voice was all nasal, like a foghorn. "It's none of your business who we bring in here. A little discretion, okay fella? The kid needs her privacy. Just leave her alone."

"Kid?" I turned to the guy who had been the soft touch for the candy bar. "That smelly pile of clothes was a kid?" I propped my foot up on Useless, but it wheeled away on me, so I had to scramble up to grab it and put the brake on. By the time I got back, Shawn's buddy — his badge read "Garth" — had clammed up, and his lips pressed together like he thought I was

25

going to steal his gum or something.

"Guys, guys — if that's a kid, I'll find out soon enough, anyway. I'm the only one in the ... the ward up there." I couldn't stand to say "Children's Ward," Abs. Hard enough having to stay here when I'm fifteen and all. You know how much I love those sticky little Winnie-the-Pooh characters half-peeling off all the walls around this place. "Just tell me what she's doing here, okay? She looked pretty rough. Get hit by a car?"

"Nah, she just fell ...," started Garth, when Shawn shot him a glance.

I tried to look encouraging to Garth, but the next thing I knew the Emerg door opened and the battleaxe who calls herself the head nurse down there was waving forms at the ambulance guys. They signed up the paperwork quick as a wink and headed for the door.

"Don't forget to give that nose a blow, Shawn," I called out at him. "Nasty little cold you're developing there!"

He fired me one last glare and was gone.

I hate that freakin' exit sign. Always glowing away up there, even if the power goes out. It's like some kind of portal for everybody else to use. Everybody but me.

So there's your journal entry for today, Abbie. And I think I should get credit for tomorrow, too, since this is like four times longer than anything I've ever written for you. English homework all sewn up, wouldn't you say? And I'm not going to tell you what that dumb-ass Garth left behind on his seat in Emerg. Let's just say the stomach-ache was worth it.

L.K.

3

"Geez, Logan. You sounded pretty upset."

Logan shrugged. Probably not a good idea to let the kid know too much of what he was thinking. "Well, you know how it is. I got over it."

Kip looked at him with those giant little-kid eyes. "I don't know about that. I remember you were still pretty mad when I got here." He pulled the notebook onto his own lap. "Look! The next bit is about Cleo. Let's read that."

Logan glanced at his watch. His stomach twisted with nerves, but he couldn't let the kid see that. He just needed to get the information he came for and get out of here.

"Just a sec, Kip. Are they doing extra bed checks on you these days? Because if that nurse comes in here and I get caught, I'm toast."

Kip shook his head. "No, we should be good for a while. I can usually manage about an extra hour of computer time in between checks at night." He grinned shyly. "I like playing that game you showed me. You know the one where you draw the line and the stick man drives along on his motorbike until he crashes?"

Logan had to smile back. At least the kid was learning. "Okay, we'll keep reading for now, but I may have to make a fast exit at some point."

He glanced down at the handwriting in the next section. The information had to be here. But if he grabbed the book and ran, the kid would turn on him. And he had to read it sometime. He couldn't make a decision without it. The kid flipped the page and Cleo's voice filled his head.

November 6
~~Cleo J.~~ Jacqueline Hornby-Moss *<SSRI — Prozac>*
<u>9:17 a.m.</u>

Good morning, Ms. Zephyr. This is my third day here at the Evergreen County Hospital, and I'm certain it will be my last. I've spent the past two days going through one test after another, each more horribly embarrassing than the one before.

I'm writing my journal here in your notebook because ... well, because you asked me to. Everyone else who works around here has just <u>told</u> me what to do, but you just seem so nice and don't act anything like that Medusa of a nurse. And of course, I will be going home soon, but just to humour you I agree to write a page or two. I hope you will appreciate the effort I have taken to design my own letterhead.

And so, Ms. Abigail Zephyr (such a nice, soft name you have), here is the information about me that you requested:

- My birth name is Cleopatra and I'm only telling you that for the sake of absolute veracity. I'm not going to put down my other names, because of course it is a mistake that I am here in the first place. And anyway, I much prefer to be called Jacqueline. Jacqueline Hornby-Moss. Isn't it lovely? You may call me that if we get close, which we likely won't since I plan on leaving here today.

- I am almost 14 — it's just a little more than three weeks until my birthday. I'm in the ninth grade at Evergreen Middle School. Skipped fourth grade, which makes me the youngest in my class. They don't usually do that anymore but in my case they made an exception. Next year will be high school, and I'll have to take a bus out of Evergreen to the big consolidated school down the freeway. I have to say I am extremely nervous about the idea of high school, but in an excited sort of way. At least some of the time.

- I'm not really comfortable discussing the reasons that I have been admitted to this place. Obviously the nurses and doctors have made a mistake. I mean, a girl gets a little dizzy at school and everyone has a fit. I did break my wrist in the fall down the stairs, but that can happen to anyone, right? Other than that I am in the prime of health. Couldn't be better.

I think that's all I can manage today, Ms. Zephyr. It's been very nice to meet you.

Sincerely,
Jacqueline Hornby-Moss.

Things to Do Today
Logan's Top 5 Cars of All Time
5. McLaren F1 1996 (silver)
4. Mercedes Benz 300 SL 1955 Gullwing (silver)
3. Bizzarini Strata 1965 (red)
2. Aston Martin DB5 1965 (silver)
1. 1961 Ferrari California (silver)
Hey Abbie,
I made this list instead of a journal today. Hope you agree with my choices.
Logan.

November 7
Jacqueline H-M. <*SSRI, Prozac, Beta Blocker, Potassium*>
<u>10:42 a.m.</u>

Dear Ms. Zephyr,

I'm afraid I find myself unable to call you by your
first name as you have requested. First, I was taught that
I must speak to older people in a formal way, so even
though you seem quite young for a teacher, I still feel
odd about it. And second, I have had a terrible blow this
morning, and I believe you might be a part of the group
working against me.

You did ask that I note down the time whenever I write
in this journal, and from that I hope you can see that
today it has taken me a great deal longer than yesterday
to get down to work. I spent the morning arguing, Ms.
Zephyr, with that Medusa of a nurse and the rest of those
professional food pushers who all seemed to want to talk
at once. There is <u>nothing</u> <u>else</u> wrong with me. It's just a
broken wrist. Anyone can have a broken wrist, especially
if they have fallen down the stairs. You can hardly walk
through the halls at school without seeing someone in a
cast for a broken arm or a broken leg. It is not only me.
Plus, I remembered this morning that I distinctly felt a
push before I fell. I'm sure now that the whole thing
was on purpose. Someone who doesn't like me at school
pushed me down the stairs. I suspect a Certain Person,

though of course I don't have the evidence to say so, and I would never dream of implicating anyone without proof. Even if she is the meanest girl in the school and would stoop to anything to get what she wants.

But when no one would believe me this morning, Ms. Zephyr, I had the single, faint hope that you would come to my aid. After all, when you asked me to participate in your tutoring session yesterday I attended more than willingly, in spite of the fact that I am here in error. I completed every assignment that you requested, including writing a journal page even though I get top marks in English and don't really need the practice.

And regardless of what could have been quality reading time that I sacrificed to complete your busy-work, you still didn't help me stand up against the doctors. I do <u>not</u> need a bone density test. My bones are fine, apart from the broken wrist, which as I have mentioned could have happened to anyone who may have had the misfortune to fall down the stairs. You did not support me, Ms. Zephyr. And the medication that Medusa has noted on the top of this page is making me sleepy and sad. I have nothing left to say except that I miss my dog Zoë and it is time for me to go home. I trust you will all come to your senses tomorrow.

Jacqueline Hornby-Moss

Evergreen Hospital
Abigail Zephyr
Evergreen Hospital Department Head, Education
Office: 101-456-7890

<u>Parental Questionnaire</u>

Requested by: Abigail Zephyr, interim teacher
To be completed by the parent of:
Cleopatra Jones

1. Please note down a brief description of your child's attitude toward school.
She loves it! A straight A student, always.

2. What are your child's general likes and dislikes?
Cleo loves everything and everybody. She is a dear child.

3. What are your child's fears, if any?
None I can think of.

4. What would you like your child to accomplish academically during his/her hospital stay?

I'm not worried at all about Cleopatra's school workload. I'm sure she will keep up her high standing while regaining her health.

5. What is your child's favourite subject at school?

Not sure. I think she enjoys all of them. She is very clever and has always done exceptionally well at school. Following in her sister's footsteps with straight A's!

6. Other concerns you feel we should know about.

None, really. Cleopatra is very self-reliant. She doesn't ever ask for help or express any worries at all.

Donna-Jay Jones

November 7
Logan K.   *<IV fluids, corticosteroids>*
<u>After lunch, which didn't resemble anything I'd call</u>
<u>food.</u>

Hey, Abbie, I can't believe you wouldn't accept my incredible vehicle list instead of writing this stupid journal today. That stinks. Just so you know, I plan to own every one of those cars one day. And I will, dude, since my dad is making a fortune working in Denver right now. He drives a pretty cool car himself. 2007 Hummer. Silver, too. All silver.

So, can you believe that new chick? A bit full of herself, in my opinion, though obviously not full of much else. I don't think I've ever seen such a pale, skinny thing in my life. She makes that Olsen twin look like a porker. She even makes me look fat!

Seems weird that they'd keep her here like that for just a broken arm, though. I heard one of the nurses say that she passed out at the top of the stairs at her school — just tipped over like a drunken monkey. I remember that staircase from when I went to Ev-Mid a couple of years ago. All cement and hard edges. No wonder her face is scraped up like that. She's lucky she didn't lose any teeth. My buddy Joe took a header off his board one day when he was cruising down a sweet pair of handrails just outside the office of the school. Unfortunately, he didn't know they'd recently put up anti-skate knobs all down the rails. Left his teeth all over the cement steps. So the skinny chick should consider herself lucky.

Maybe they're keeping her here because she got some internal injury.

Who cares? I can hardly stand to hear her talk. She's totally stuck up and wants to put everyone down by using words normal people have never heard of. Besides, she said she's probably out of here tomorrow. Sayonara, sweetheart. Can't say it's been nice knowing you.

Logan

WHILE YOU WERE OUT

Abbie Z,

Please page Rena Cordula, Transplant Program Coordinator, at #195, regarding a patient transfer.

Thx,
Karna, Reception

November 7
Logan K.　　　　　*< IV fluids, corticosteroids>*
<u>9 p.m. Primetime. Just what are you thinking, Abbie?</u>

Geez, Abster. I'm missing all the good shows.
You've never made me do homework this late. And
you know what? This caf stinks at night. All I can smell
is the grease from the cooking, if that's what you call
what they do down here. French fry grease and Lysol.
It reeks, dude.

Okay, I know I was a little hard on the chick. So
I'm sorry already. You can appreciate that I don't really
know her — I was just commenting on what I could
see, right? But I want to get back to the TV, so here
goes. And by the way, you can say goodbye to the
remote. I'm hiding it tomorrow.

Okay, the chick with the scraped face and the broken
arm is probably a good person because ... ah ... because ...

Abbie, this is so stupid. I can't think of anything to
say. I don't even know her, for crissakes. She's just some
stupid, skinny chick.

Okay, I just thought of something. She didn't give me
that better-be-nice-to-the-kid-maybe-he's-dying look.
So there you go. I like her better already.

One other thing. Did you know you're named after a
very cool car? I just pulled it off the internet this morning
to add to the list of vehicles I plan to have in my garage
some day. Here's a sketch of what it looks like:

Evergreen Hospital
Children's Ward – Desk 9
Office: 101-456-7890

November 7

To: Ms. Abigail Zephyr
      Evergreen Hospital,
      Education Department Head

Re: In-hospital school work schedule change

Dr. Valens has requested that Logan Kemp be withdrawn from any schoolwork tomorrow morning, due to a scheduled series of blood tests. The doctor reports that the anticipated increase in medication may leave the patient moody or depressed. He asks that you report any symptoms to him directly.

Thank you.

Takehiko Ken, RN.

Dr. Rob Valens
Evergreen Family Medicine
Office: 101-456-7890

November 8

To: Ms. Abigail Zephyr
Evergreen Hospital,
Education Department Head

PRIVATE & CONFIDENTIAL

Re: Your call regarding Logan Kemp

Regarding the message you left on my voice mail earlier today, I have decided to make a change in Logan Kemp's medications. His condition has only responded in a limited manner to treatment. I have noted your comments about his increasing despondency and displays of anger, and have adjusted his medication accordingly. Please continue to monitor and feel free to call me at any time should he begin exhibiting any further symptoms.

Rob Valens, MD.

November 8
Logan K.   *<IV fluids, corticosteroids>*
<u>After some kind of disgusting liquid breakfast.</u>

Okay, Abbie, I'm gonna make this quick today. My face has gone all puffy and gross, obviously from the toxic cocktail these creeps are pouring into my veins through Useless here. And I did extra math for you, remember? That's gotta count for something. Sorry ... it has got to count for something. Is that better? Because I know you're trying to improve my grammar by giving me this freakin' journal to write, but lady — it ain't gonna happen. (Ha — just a joke, of course. You always have such a great sense of humour, Abbie. And nice hair, too. Did I mention the nice hair?)

Anyway, I just looked it up and the dictionary says a paragraph can contain a minimum of three sentences. I do believe the above paragraph qualifies, and therefore, in the words of Carl Sagan, I am outta here!

L.K.

From the Desk of Donna-Fay Jones

Dear Ms. Zephyr,

It was lovely to meet you in person today at last. I'm so sorry I had to rush away — my elder daughter had a small emergency. She has a final audition for a position as a line dancer at the Starlight Dinner Theatre later this week. The dress we had lined up for her required alterations and the seamstress was only available today.

I know my baby will work hard and do her best for you, Ms. Zephyr. I don't know how the situation with her appetite went downhill so fast. Cleopatra and food just never have gotten along. She was a fussy eater as a baby and she still is. It has never been a problem before. I just want you to know that this child is well-loved and no one in her family has ever encouraged this sort of behaviour in the slightest. Thank you for your help with Cleopatra.

Sincerely,
Donna-Fay Jones

P.S. I remember a girl from Atlanta in one of Helena's early pageant events whose last name was Zephyr (or perhaps Zimmer). Do you have any family in Atlanta? D-F J.

"Wow," said Logan. "I'm such an idiot."

"What's wrong?"

Logan stared at the notebook. "If I'd paid more attention to some of the stuff in this book, I would have clued in to some things a lot sooner."

Kip looked at him quizzically. "What kind of things? I never read any of the other stuff in there, Logan. It's just a place to put my work for Abbie."

Logan turned back to the notebook, avoiding Kip's eyes.

"Just things," he muttered, and turned to the next page.

November 8

Logan K.   *<IV fluids, corticosteroids>*

<u>Back in the stinking cafeteria after all the cows have gone home.</u>

Okay, so I was wrong. No sense of humour whatsoever. Still like your hair, though.

And I was *not* trying to get out of doing my work. I did my work — I wrote a paragraph, just like you said. It's just that I've been here for over a week now. And there you are every day, bugging me to get my schoolwork

43

done. I feel lousy, all right? Are you happy to hear me admit it? Last week when I got here, I thought it might just be for overnight. And don't tell me that makes me have something in common with the little weirdie down the hall, because it doesn't.

When Tom tossed the ball at me in practice, he didn't even throw it that hard, but when I caught it and everybody piled on me in the scrum, I suddenly felt like a bomb had gone off in my gut. I just managed to pull myself out of the pile and run like a madman off the field and straight into the changing room. I'm still falling on my knees every night to thank God I made it to the can. There was blood everywhere and it was obvious something inside me was seriously messed up. But Abbie, I thought it was just because I fell on the rugby ball. Off to the hospital. Stitch me up, fix whatever made me bleed like that, send me home. Was I ever wrong.

Anyway, I don't want to write about it anymore. These drugs seem to finally be kicking in and my gut doesn't hurt quite as bad. We've got a big meeting happening tomorrow — the doc, the nutritionist, my parents. (Actually, it turns out my dad's really busy and can't make it in from Denver, but everybody else will be there.) So, much as I like your hair, Teach, I'll be happy to bid you and the little weirdie down the hall AND this stupid journal goodbye.

L.K.

Evergreen Middle School: Interim Report

PRIVATE AND CONFIDENTIAL

Student Name: Cleopatra Jones   Grade: 9
Date: November 8

This report is intended to pass formal information ONLY regarding the above-mentioned student to temporary teacher **Ms. Abigail Zephyr** in the subject of **English 9**.

Punctuality 0 lates   Attendance 0 absences
(perfect attendance)

Classroom marks to date:

Test 1	Sept 9	assessment	98.8%	A
Test 2	Sept 27	grammar	100%	A
Test 3	Oct 5	in-class essay	93%	A
Test 4	Oct 16	comprehension	90%	A
Test 5	Oct 29	parts of speech	100%	A

Cleo is a model student, though I worry she takes things a bit too seriously. Her work standard is excellent.

Teacher Name: **Ellie Plato, English Department**

November 11
Jacqueline H-M. *<SSRI, Paxil, Beta Blocker, Potassium>*
<u>9:11 a.m.</u>

Good morning, Ms. Zephyr. I say that strictly out of
good manners and because of your kind offer to take
dictation for me. (As you can see, I am managing just fine
with my left hand. But thank you anyway.)

There is nothing else good about this morning. This
place is worse than even my real school. That Logan is *so*
mean. He calls me a "little weirdie." Please! Who is the
weird one? And he's always talking about your hair. Have
you seen *his* hair? It's so thick and curly it really needs to
either be cut short or at the very least *brushed* occasionally.
Just because a person is six feet tall is no reason for not
brushing his hair. Newsflash: we can all still see it from
down here. He looks like a giant brunette dandelion.

And he has horrifying etiquette. I understand he
hasn't been able to eat for a while. He certainly looks
out of practice. He has the table manners of a warthog.
In fact, I watched him stuff some kind of candy down
his throat when we were watching television last night.
You can find the wrappers under the couch cushions, if
you are interested.

But Logan aside, I am trying to be patient, Ms. Zephyr,
though it is difficult when so many people around here
want to keep touching me. I spent most of yesterday
afternoon hooked up to some kind of heart monitor.

I hate that thing, and besides, it doesn't seem to work properly. That Nurse Hydra insists that my heartbeat is irregular. How ridiculous is that? Anyway, as a result, I am sorry to say that I did not get my math questions finished. I will get them done tonight, I promise. I can't stand another evening in the company of Mr. Kemp, anyway.

The best thing about you, Ms. Zephyr, is that you seem to be able to talk to me without feeling compelled to take my temperature or my blood pressure. I'm grateful for that, believe me. And I still hold out hope that you can drop even a tiny hint to the doctor that I am doing very well. Even my mother can't get the doctor to see reason. She knows I am fine. I agree that I may be a little pale these days but that is no reason to keep me hooked up to these machines.

Oh no ... here comes Nurse Medusa to force one of those awful protein bars down my throat. This will have to be all for today.

Jacqueline H-M.

From the desk of...

Abigail Zephyr
Evergreen Hospital
Department Head, Education
Office: 101-456-7890

Abbie,

I can't find you anywhere, so I stole some of your paper from the nurses' station to leave you a note. First off, I found out this morning that there are no plans to let me out of here anytime soon. And on top of that I just heard what makes that little weird chick tick ... or not tick as seems to have just happened. You must have known what's wrong. Why didn't you tell me? Scared I'd go in and scream at her or rip her fool head off?

And just ignore that hole that I kicked through your office wall. Or better still, consider it my homework for today. I think you might be busy seeing the little weirdie through her self-induced heart-failure.

Maybe someone that stupid <u>deserves</u> to die.

Logan

4

Logan didn't want to look at the kid. He could feel the bed shaking a little and he knew Kip was crying.

"I didn't really mean it," he said, without looking up. "I was upset, okay?"

"Cleo's not stupid, Logan. She was just a bit mixed up, is all. But nobody deserves to die when they are a kid, Logan. Nobody."

Logan felt like he was going to choke on all the different feelings that were battling in his throat. Here he was, arguing about dying with a kid hooked up to the latest in medical miracle machines. This was the last thing he wanted to talk about with Kip right now. But he needed answers and he needed them fast.

He jumped off the bed.

"Okay, so you're right, already. No kid deserves to die. And I shouldn't have kicked the wall in, either. But I was mad. I was mad that someone who had everything going for her was so messed up. But now I'm not just mad, I'm worried."

"Well, I'm worried, too," said Kip, wiping his face with the back of one hand.

They were both quiet a moment, listening to the

various beeps and hums in the room. Kip reached out and pulled the notebook closer.

"I forgot about the *Jacqueline* name," he said, smiling a little. "Cleo is crazy, right?"

Logan didn't know what to say. "I hope not," he muttered.

Kip looked up at him through tired eyes. "How come you're reading this stuff to me, Logan? You've never read anything to me before. Lots of computer games, but no books."

Logan stuck his finger in the notebook to mark his place and took a quick glance out the window into the hall. No nurses in sight. But the clock was still ticking and the kid kept asking awkward questions. He closed the notebook and slid off the bed.

"Look, dude. I wish I could tell you, but I can't. Someone's in trouble and I need to find them, all right? And I think something in the notebook might help me do that. That's all I can tell you right now, okay?"

The kid stared at him a moment and then reached over to the table to grab his laptop.

"I know more than you think I do," he said quietly. "I think you're trying to rescue Cleo."

Logan swallowed, his throat feeling suddenly dry. This was really bad news. If this eleven-year-old kid was onto him, could the cops be far behind? He checked the window again compulsively and then moved back to sit on the corner of Kip's bed.

"Why do you think Cleo needs rescuing, Kip?"

The LED lights blinked green and red in the darkness above the bed and one of the machines clicked regularly. *Heart monitor*, Logan thought.

"I can't tell you," Kip said after a long pause. "But maybe I can show you."

He leaned forward and pulled the notebook out of Logan's hand.

November 11

Kip Graeme   *<immune suppressant, corticosteroids, analgesic>*

Hi Abbie!

Long time no write! I'm back again — your fave Kidney Kid. This time I'm in the hospital for just one week. Dr. Robbie says I need just a quick clean-out of my blood and then I can go home. Not like last year, huh? Dr. Robbie says I should be careful so I don't get that sick again; it's my job to look after my new kidney.

You have a different notebook this time, but I bet you kept your old one, right? I remember how you want me to stick my journal entries and math in here, just like before. But remember, last year you made me write about where I live and my vacation and all that. I hope you've still got all that stuff in your old book because I don't want to write it all out again. So I can just skip it, right? The only difference is that now I am eleven and last year I was ten. Same everything else.

This year, I suppose you'll want me to write about how it feels to be back. It feels not too bad. Well, not as bad as I thought, anyway. I only have to stay a week this time. I get to skip school, too, so not a bad deal. Besides, school with you is easier. Plus there's no one to bug me about my fat face or anything.

Things seem the same around here. A little quieter than last summer, maybe. Remember Spencer? He was that kid who broke his back and his leg doing wheelies on his ATV. Anyway, I saw him last night when I was in Emerg. This time he has a broken arm. He got it riding his bike along a fence. Guess he forgot about fence posts.

Okay, Abbie, that's a whole page, so I am done for today. I checked my spelling, and I think I got all the mistakes out, too.

From,
Kip.

Evergreen Middle School: E-mail

To: Abbie Zephyr <a_zephyr@evergreen.org>
From: Ellie Plato <e_plato@ems.sd45.us.org>
Re: Catching UP!

Hi Abbie –

Hey girlfriend! I think the last time we talked was at the professional development conference two years ago in Chicago — remember? We had to sit and listen to that intensely boring school board guy for what seemed like hours. Don't know how I would have survived it if I hadn't had you to exchange disparaging notes with. I was glad to see the inside of the hotel bar after that long day, I can tell you. ;)

Just thought I'd drop you a line today to say "hi" in addition to the formal report I sent through the mail. I had no idea you'd given up your position at Cartwright to teach in the hospital. That's got to be so hard — you have my sympathies. I can barely stand the little buggers in the classroom — dealing with them in a hospital setting would be way more than I could cope with. Speaking of which, best of luck with Cleopatra Jones. Bit of an eccentric kid there, as you've probably already figured out. She drives me crazy correcting my grammar in class, but at least she's a hard worker.

Guess this hospital stay explains why she was always dragging around in that huge red sweater. I heard they had to unwrap ten layers of clothes from the poor thing when she fell. I just don't get how kids can do these things to themselves.

You'll have read my formal report already, so you know her marks are great. I knew something was up with the kid but I have a group of six real winners in that class so I didn't really have time to waste on Cleopatra. It's all I can do to keep the Gang of Six in their desks and out of trouble. A week ago, one of them held a match to my favourite "Reading Rules" poster. (It has a picture of a French poodle. Very cute.) Anyway, the kid nearly burnt the classroom down. Whole school evacuated, of course, but only a little smoke damage in the end. The poster was destroyed, naturally. It actually turned out well, because now that he's expelled I only have five monsters to deal with in that class.

Definitely worth the loss of the poster. I should write a book.

Anyway, I hope things turn around for Cleopatra. And hey, let's get together sometime for a drink.

A bunch of the staff meet up Fridays at the road-house in Clearwater — we can avoid both the parents and the kids that way. Come and meet us sometime. I'd love to see you again.

Ellie

November 12
Jacqueline H-M *<antiarrhythmic, gastric feeding tube>*
<u>Can't see a clock and someone has taken my watch.</u>

Dear Ms. Zephyr,

I don't feel very well so I will not be terribly prolific today. Some little kid keeps knocking at my door. I wish somebody would tell him I don't even know how to play poker.

The only good thing out of all this mess is that Medusa has to stop forcing food on me now. My throat is terribly sore from this tube, though. Hopefully I will never see another one of those vile protein shakes as long as I live. Which is going to be a long time, Abbie. My Nona is almost 80 and she is doing just fine. She's pretty skinny, too, but she doesn't have heart problems. <u>Neither do I.</u> I did NOT have a heart attack. Dr. Valens says my heart "just fluttered a bit," which I am sure is simply another way to say I had a fainting spell. Anyone

55

can have a fainting spell. Especially in the hospital. You would think this would be a <u>good</u> place to faint, since it gives everybody a chance to practice their craft.

I'm sure I'll feel better tomorrow. And I'll catch up on my homework, too, I promise. I just need to sleep for a while.   ~~Cleo.~~ Jacqueline

Hi Abbie,

It's ten o'clock and you are not here so I'm writing you a note cause something bad happened. I'm worried about that skinny girl who says her name is not Cleopatra, even though the sign on her door says it is. When I got here I went in to say "hi," but she looked pretty sad. I remember how sad I was when my kidney stopped working and I had an operation. So I tried to cheer the girl up but it didn't work. She yelled that her name was Jacklin and not Cleopatra and said I was an idiot. Then she threw her math book at me. It hit the TV and knocked it off the stand. The TV broke on the floor and Nurse Taki came in and yelled. And the girl just curled up in her bed and looked worse than ever. I said sorry to her and sorry to Nurse Taki but I think they are both mad at me now. I wish my mom was here. She would fix everything.

Kip

November 13
Logan K.   *<IV fluids, corticosteroids>*
<u>Too early.</u>

Hey Abster,

Sorry about your office wall. I was feeling pretty mad and crazy and down, and that new kid was driving me nuts. It was kick the wall or the kid. So the wall got it. Crappy walls around here, Abbie. Didn't hurt my foot and I wasn't even wearing my Doc Martens.

Nurse Takehiko was pretty pissed with me. Apparently the little weirdie smashed a TV set today, too, so looks like parental-payout time around here. These destructive teenagers, eh? And I never knew what hospital cutbacks were before today. No wonder this place always looks so dingy. Anyway, I helped Ramone (the janitor dude) repair the damage. He wasn't so happy with me, I have to say, but at least we got the work done. But he said his union would kill him if they saw some kid passing him his tools or whatever, so we can't tell anyone, okay?

And, in case you don't believe me, I <u>am</u> sorry.

I still don't get the little weirdie, though. No wonder she's breaking TV sets — she must be really crazy. What kind of idiot starves herself into the hospital? And into heart failure? I hear it wasn't a real heart attack, actually. Takehiko said she just went into fibrillation or something like that. Not enough potassium or something.

So how stupid are the staff around here? I guess you people don't have enough to do or something. It's an easy cure: stuff the chick with some decent food (I recommend pizza) and send her home. Problem solved.

Logan

To: a_zephyr@evergreen.org
From: tommykixa$$@coldlist.com

_____

Hey Ms. Zephyr.

I hope I have the right person here. My name is Tom Juwell. I can't seem to get ahold of a buddy of mine. His name is Logan Kemp. Coach told us he's in the hospital, but since I am not in his family they won't give me any information. I got your e-mail from the hospital website. Hey, can you just tell him to call me or something? The guys on the team all heard he was sick so we sent him a card. But I'd like to hear how he's doing so I was hoping you could get him to call me. Or e-mail would be good, too.

Thanks.
Tom

Evergreen Hospital
Children's Ward – Desk 9
Office: 101-456-7890

November 14

To: Ms. Abigail Zephyr
    Evergreen Hospital Education
    Department Head

Re: Call from Angela Kemp (Logan Kemp's mother), 1:40 a.m.

Message: Sorry to call so late. Stuck @ Black & White Ball until wee hours this evening. Just found Logan's school binder under his bed. Will send to hosp. tomorrow a.m. by messenger. My apologies — thought he had it with him. No need to call back.

Message taken by:
T. Ken, RN.

November 14
Logan K.   *<corticosteroids>*
<u>Before lunch and too early to be working</u>

Hey, Abbie, I don't have to use my school binder in here, do I? It has all kinds of other stuff from the beginning of the year and we're not doing any of the same things now, anyway. I hate looking at it. It reminds me of when I wasn't sick. Pretty lame that my mom just found it now — I left it right at the bottom of my bed. I guess she's not sitting in there at night moaning over the loss of her absent son.

It's okay, I'd rather talk about the team. You did say today's writing topic was about our friends, right? They sent me the card in my room — did you see it? Coach called me, too. He says the team is too loud to come in to see me, but they've dedicated practice to me a couple of times. That rocks. I just wish I was there. I could kick some serious butt right now. I'm so sick of being here I could puke.

Thanks for passing on Tom's e-mail. I can use that internet station at the end of the hall to e-mail him back. Not that I want to tell him about anything happening around here. This place sucks. But I'd like to hear how the team is doing with pre-season and all. I plan to be back on that field the day I finally get out of here. I can't wait.

Logan

November 14
Logan K.   *<corticosteroids>*
<u>After lunch.</u>

I thought you might like to look at a bit of the graphic novel I was working on for my English class before I got stuck in here. So this should count for a journal entry, right?

Many millennia in the past, a stagnant swamp festers under the heat of a sweltering sun...

But still waters may hide deep secrets....

BLACK, BLACK & KEMP
ATTORNEYS-AT-LAW
3600 MESA BOULEVARD | DENVER, CO | 555.555.1234

To: Ms. Abigail Zephyr
    Department Head, Hospital Education
    Evergreen Hospital

Date: November 12

Re: Logan Kemp

Dear Ms. Zephyr,

I am writing to you on behalf of Mr. Carter
Kemp, the father of a patient of yours, Logan
Kemp. Further to his thoughts as presented in
the teleconference meeting with you last week,
Mr. Kemp Senior is very concerned that Logan
be encouraged by every means possible to
maintain his studies while hospitalized.

Mr. Carter Kemp has asked me to assure you
that his investigation into your teaching history
uncovered impeccable credentials including a
very favourable reference on your record by
New York financier Harold Stump. He insists

you know he has every faith in your capabilities as a teacher.

He would also like you to be aware that he has extremely high hopes for Logan Kemp as a candidate for the Heineken-Europa scholarship to Branson Prep, Mr. Kemp Senior's own undergraduate alma mater. You may be aware that prior to graduating *summa cum laude* from Harvard Law School, Mr. Carter Kemp was an all-star rugby player in his first year at Branson Prep.

He trusts you understand the importance of preparing Logan for a successful experience with the preliminary entrance and scholarship exams, scheduled for the end of Logan's junior year in May.

Your attention to these matters is most appreciated.

Sincerely,
Francine Peon-Anderson
Senior Administrative Assistant to
Mr. Carter Logan, BSc MBA LLB LLM

3600 MESA BOULEVARD | DENVER, CO | 555.555.1234

5

"I hate reading all this crap about me," Logan muttered, tossing the notebook down. He leaned back and rubbed his eyes. "*Extremely high hopes,*" the letter had said. Right. He could just imagine what his dad was thinking now. Mr. Carter Kemp, the all-star rugby player, now with some kind of a diseased wimp for a son. He'd probably not even trouble himself to make the trip from Denver anymore. Why bother? He usually only showed up for games, anyway.

Kip looked down at the notebook again. "It's harder to find the stuff I want to show you in here than I thought. Abbie keeps all our work mixed together."

Logan sighed. "I know. You'd think as a teacher she'd be more organized."

"I think the notebook helps her stay organized," said Kip. "But I wanted you to see that Cleo was getting better. Everybody thought she was."

"I know," said Logan. "I believed it, too. But now I'm not so sure."

Kip pushed himself up a little higher in the bed. He shot Logan a funny look.

"I did think she was getting better," he said quietly, "but

running away is just going to makes things much worse."

The room was silent, with the muted beep and clunk of the machines sounding suddenly loud by contrast.

After a moment, Logan realized that his mouth was actually gaping in surprise.

"You know? You've known all this time that she's run away?"

Kip nodded. "I found out she was going, but she made me promise not to tell."

Logan closed his eyes and leaned against the wall with a groan. "And here I thought you would go straight to the nurses if you found out she was gone," he said. He opened his eyes and looked at Kip, sitting upright and wide awake in his bed in spite of the hour. "You're more trustworthy than I thought, kid."

Kip smiled a little at this. "Cleo knew I wouldn't tell," he said. He shifted uncomfortably in his bed. "But I'm really scared for her, Logan. Besides, everybody will figure out she's gone pretty quickly, I think. There are no secrets around here."

Logan strode around to the head of the bed. "You're right, Kip. But I think you and I are looking for the same thing here. We just want to make sure Cleo is safe, right?"

Kip nodded slowly. "I guess so. But she did ask me not to tell anybody anything. And that would include you, Logan."

Logan leaned on the table and stuck his nose right in Kip's face. "Look, kid. Time is passing. Cleo is gone and, unless she told you more than she told me, we don't know where. We need to work together to make sure she's safe. So here's the deal: we both know you're stuck in this bed, but there is still a way for you to help. Now what did Cleo say to you?"

As he leaned forward encouragingly, one of his fingers caught on the wire leading to the heart monitor, pinching it between his palm and the corner of the table. The machine's alarm howled and a red light above the door began to flash.

* * *

Logan waited a full five minutes after the sound of Nurse Takehiko's shoes receded in the distance before crawling out from under the bed. His eyes had adjusted to the dark from lying under the bed all that time, and in the glow of the flashing lights he could see Kip was grinning broadly.

"That was awesome, Logan. I never knew you could move so fast."

Logan rubbed his head where he'd smacked it on the steel strut under the bed. "Neither did I."

He sat back down on the bed, gingerly avoiding any wire or tube he could see. "Dude, that thing was loud. I thought she'd catch me for sure."

"Me too. But I'm glad she didn't. You would have been in so much trouble. But it was okay. I just told her

I must have rolled over on it in my sleep."

Logan nodded and squeezed a button on his watch. The face glowed blue in the dark room. "Yeah, I know. Listen, Kip. I've got to get out of here."

"But I thought you wanted to hear about what Cleo had to say."

"Well, yeah, I do. But you need to tell me quick and without any more alarms ringing. I'm going to be the one who needs a heart monitor if that thing goes off again." Logan leaned forward and flipped on the tiny lamp that the nurses used for reading charts at night.

"Okay, okay." But Kip just fidgeted with his laptop.

Logan could feel impatience surging inside him like a rising helium balloon.

Kip finally broke his silence. "She said she had filled out a transfer form and that the nurses would think she was in the psych ward. She said by the time they figured it out, she would have a chance to do what she had to do." He bit his lip. "But she wouldn't tell me where she was going, Logan. Do you know where she's gone?"

Logan shrugged. "Maybe. I know about the transfer form, anyway. I helped her steal the thing, for crissakes." He shook his head. "Looks like she was using us both, dude."

"There's something else." Kip leaned over and pulled a small pill bottle from the drawer in his bedside table. "She forgot this."

Logan took it and held the label up to the lamp. His

insides coalesced into a cold, hard lump. She left without her meds. Maybe his worst fears were true.

"Doesn't she need her medicine, Logan? She left here so fast and all her stuff is still in her drawer."

Logan swallowed. Her meds and all her stuff left behind? This was not good. NOT good. But Kip didn't need to know how bad things really were. The kid had enough to worry about. Let him think that Cleo was just running away. Time to play it cool.

He raised his eyebrows at Kip. "How do you know what was in her drawer? She'll hit the roof if she finds out you went through her things."

Kip's eyes widened. "Hey, I'm not crazy. She just left that bottle on her table. I didn't even touch her drawer. But if she'd really been transferred, they'd have sent her medicine with her, wouldn't they? They would have gathered up all her stuff in a bag and sent it along with her. So they might miss the stuff in the drawers for a day or two, but if the nurses see this, they'll figure out something is wrong."

Logan smiled a little as he pocketed the pills. "Good thinking kid. I'll make sure she gets these. So, did you try to talk her out of going?"

"I didn't really say much. Just made her promise to ..."

"Promise to what, dude?"

Kip shot him a sceptical glance and tucked the laptop a little further under the covers.

"Listen, I don't have time for this, kid. If Cleo is your

friend you should tell me if you know anything about where she's gone. I'm not going to force her to come home or anything. I won't tell anyone else. I just want to make sure she's all right and to ... well, I have to give her something."

Logan looked at Kip in the dim glow of the chart lamp. Just a little kid with big eyes and a bunch of wires connecting him to all the hospital paraphernalia. Usually he was immune to all those cute kid things — save it for the commercials, for crissakes — but maybe this was different. After all, he knew something of what living with pain was like. He'd been there. He likely would be there again. And Kip just wanted to help. He tried again.

"Kip, you know I won't do anything to hurt Cleo. I promise. I know she's your friend, but I'm your friend, too, right? I taught you how to play *Halo*, dude — that's gotta count for something."

Kip stared back at Logan for a long, silent moment, and then slid the laptop out from under the covers. "Okay, but I can only tell you a little. I'm not going to break my promise to Cleo."

He flipped open the lid of the laptop and Logan saw to his surprise that instead of a computer game, Kip was in the middle of composing a letter on his e-mail account.

Return address: *JH-M@coldlist.com*

Logan's heart gave a little flip in his chest. Her e-mail address! But why would she give it to the kid and not to him?

"Geez, Kip, you've got to be joking. You've been talking to her by e-mail tonight?"

Kip closed the computer again and pulled it protectively onto his lap. "Not tonight, actually. She isn't on-line right now. But I know what she's doing and why she's doing it. And she promised to keep in touch with me so I would know she was all right."

Logan jammed his hands in his pockets and tried to think. Maybe things weren't as bad as he thought. Maybe Cleo had just bolted for a day or two, and she'd be back soon and everything would go back to normal. And yet ...

His fingers tested the pill bottle in his pocket. She left without her meds. But worse — she left without taking any of her stuff, which meant that she knew she wouldn't need any of it ever again. Any way he looked at it, Cleo was in trouble. And he was sitting in here, wasting time, trying to keep this little kid from talking.

"She probably only gave you the address because you're too young to do anything about it," he muttered to himself. He lifted his head and looked at Kip as though he'd never seen him before. "How old are you, Kip? Like nine or something?"

For the first time in Logan's memory Kip looked really annoyed. He drew himself up in bed. "I'm eleven, Logan. Nearly eleven and a half, actually. I'm just small for my age because ... well, just because." He looked up and Logan could see he was close to tears. "We can't all be giants, you know."

Suddenly, Logan felt terrible. Here was this little kid who probably cared about Cleo as much as he did, or even more, truth be told, *and* he was a computer whiz. New possibilities clicked through his brain. Keeping carefully away from any of Kip's equipment, Logan began to pace the floor at the end of the bed.

"Listen, dude, I'm sorry. I didn't mean to say you were small — only that for a kid so small you have a really big brain."

Kip's eyes welled up again.

"Wait, that didn't come out right. I just mean … don't be upset. This is a chance for us to work together, y'know?"

"Like that time you said we could work together on the TV, but I ended up missing my show 'cause you wanted to play Xbox? I don't want to work together like that."

"Nah, forget about that time. That was the old Logan, kid. Things are different now. At least, I'm trying to make them different. And right now, the biggest problem we have is time. We need to find out where she's going *now*. And since she's not going to tell us, we've got to figure it out ourselves."

"Do you think she'd just go home, you know, to be in her own bed?" said Kip. "I really miss my own bed. That's what I'd do."

Logan bit back a sharp retort. He had to remember the kid was only trying to help.

"Not a chance, buddy. I think you're right that she's looking for something that's important to her. I mean, it's a big risk to run away, especially when ..."

"When what?"

"When you ... uh ... know what big trouble you are going to get in if you are caught." Logan grabbed the notebook and stuck it into the tiny circle of light made by the chart lamp. "I just need some kind of clue as to where she's going. It's got to be in here."

Kip lay back against his pillow, and yawned cavernously. "Well, I still think she'd want to go where somebody loves her," he said sleepily.

Logan nearly dropped Abbie's notebook. He reached over and grabbed one of Kip's feet under the covers.

Kip's eyes flew open. "Hey!" he said indignantly.

"Listen, kid, I think you've got something. Who is the one person Cleo loves most in the world?"

"Her grandma," Kip said promptly. "And her dog, Zoë."

Logan rapidly flipped through the notebook. "She wrote something about her grandma, Kip. I know it's in here somewhere ..."

November 14
Kip G.   <immune suppressant>

Dear Abbie,

You said my journal entry for today should be about my friends. At school I don't have too many friends. Sometimes the other kids don't get why I can't play rocket dodgeball or anything, and it's hard to hang out with kids if you want to play rocket dodgeball but you can't. So, today I'm writing about the kids at the hospital here who are my friends.

The best thing about this place is that there are other kids around. Some aren't very friendly, but some are. Like Spencer from last year. He was pretty friendly. Except that time he punched me for talking too much. But mostly he was friendly.

There are two other kids in here right now, plus a baby in ICU, but that isn't our ward so it doesn't count. I tried to talk to the girl yesterday but I think she was sleepy. She doesn't like poker, that's for sure. I checked her door again. It says her name is Cleopatra, but she said that for the last time didn't I know that almost everyone here is an idiot and they got her name wrong and would I get lost. So I tried to talk to the other guy, but he was busy with the janitor patching the big hole he kicked in the wall of your office.

At least I can tell you what he looks like. He's a bit

73

scary looking. His name is Logan. He had white dust in his hair from the work he and the janitor were doing, and he is at least seven feet tall, so he must be a teenager. He seems cool, but he was very mad about having to fix the wall, so I left. I hate getting punched.

And that's it. Two kids plus me.

From,
Kip.

November 14
Jacqueline H-M.   *<antidepressant, antiarrhythmic>*
<u>5:17 p.m.</u>

Dear Ms. Zephyr,

For my journal entry today I am writing to protest the withholding of my homework. I assure you, three days is more than enough recovery time from a minor fainting spell. As you know, it was NOT a heart attack. I am very ready to get back to work. Please relent.

Oh, and while I am down on my metaphorical knees, could you also help arrange the return of my red sweater? It's always freezing in here. Thank you.

Yours impatiently,
Jacqueline

November 14
Jacqueline H-M.   *\<antiarrhythmic\>*
<u>6:04 p.m.</u>

Dear Ms. Zephyr,

I have just completed the final page of <u>Moby Dick</u> and in addition to having no homework to work on, I now officially have nothing to read. As it seems you have gone home for the day, and I can't even locate an old Reader's Digest in this godforsaken place, I will be forced to read the contents of this notebook.

Jacqueline

Evergreen Hospital
X-Ray and Laboratory Services
Office: 101-456-7890

November 14

To: Ms. Abigail Zephyr,
   Evergreen Hospital,
   Education Department Head

Re: In-hospital school work schedule change

Dr. Valens has requested that Kip Graeme be withdrawn from any schoolwork tomorrow morning, due to a scheduled series of blood tests. Kip will be able to resume full activity by tomorrow afternoon. Thank you.

S. Isaacs, Lab Tech.

November 15
Jacqueline H-M.   *<antidepressant, antiarrhythmic>*
8:59 a.m.

Dearest Ms. Zephyr,

Thank you so much for relenting! I will start on the math that I have missed right away. Will have it in to you by this afternoon, a full day before it is due, I hope you note!

However, I have another request to make. Due to your slow acquiescence on the homework front, I read all the way through this notebook. I must say I am feeling quite hurt by Mr. Kemp's journal entries. Could you please ask Mr. Kemp to cease referring to me as "the little weirdie"? First of all, "weirdie" is not a word. My name is Jacqueline Hornby-Moss. He may refer to me as Ms. Hornby-Moss or even Ms. Jacqueline if his tiny brain can't manage the whole thing.

And secondly, though I am indeed physically smaller than he is, I am most assuredly not little. Adine Terrepini at my school wears a size zero and I wear at least a size three — higher on my fat days. And not only that, I checked Mr. Kemp's chart when he was playing Xbox (as usual) and discovered that he is a mere fifteen months my senior. Less than a year and a half is hardly enough to give him such a superiority complex.

Thank you for allowing me to redress this misunderstanding.

~Jacqueline Hornby-Moss

Postscript: Ms. Zephyr, when you <u>do</u> have the opportunity to speak with Mr. Kemp, you might also mention to him that Carl Sagan would say no such thing as "I'm outta here"? I speak from experience as he was an acquaintance of our family and, according to my Nona, he was a deeply thoughtful man.

Dr. Rob Valens
Evergreen Family Medicine
Office: 101-456-7890

November 15

To: Ms. Abigail Zephyr
Evergreen Hospital Education
Department Head

Re: Recommendation regarding course methodology for patient

Regarding your question about Kip Graeme's schoolwork, I must say I am in hearty agreement about allowing him to use his laptop computer in the hospital. As I mentioned to you on the telephone yesterday, his blood tests indicate that his renal function is rapidly deteriorating and I have a very real concern that he may reach a crisis point in the next short while if the response to meds does not improve. Any action we can take with his school work to redirect his attention from the additional daily blood testing will be a welcome distraction, I am sure.

Rob Valens, MD.

November 15
Logan K.   *<corticosteroids>*
<u>Noonish</u>

Hey Abs,

Finally broke down and talked to the new kid with the kidney problem. Friendly little guy, but a bit of a pest. I hadn't known him sixty seconds before he was showing me his scar. I guess when it's emergency surgery they just slice your whole side open to get that thing out, huh?

I felt kinda sorry for the kid after that, plus I remembered I hadn't done my journal entry for today, so I took a few notes. (Hey, you can get back up off the floor, Abbie. I am only joking.)

Anyways, here's the scoop for you because we all know — repeat after me, children — a completed journal entry means unrestricted TV, right? Right.

Me: What's your name, kid?
KK: Kip. But around here, people call me the Kidney Kid.
Me: That's pretty stupid.
KK: I was born with only one kidney that didn't work so well. And I think it's because my name is Kip. It's like three Ks, right? Kip the Kidney Kid.
Me: Oh, God.

KK: Oh, sorry Logan, are you in pain? <looks worried>

Me: Uh — it's okay. When you leave it'll pass.

KK: You're pretty funny, Logan. How tall are you anyway? I guess seven feet. Want to see my scar?

Me: That's too many questions, kid. And I'm only six foot one.

KK: Wow. Six foot one is pretty tall. Do you call Jacqueline "kid" too?

Me: No. Her I call "Weird." Because she is. She's a little like you, kid.

KK: Uh, thanks.

Me: And I think I hear her calling you.

KK: Really? Maybe she wants to play poker.

Me: Oh yeah, I heard her say that. You'd better go see her right away.

KK: Okay. Bye, Logan.

Me: Nice scar, by the way.

KK: Thanks, dude.

Me: Don't call me dude. Get outta here.

And that's it, Abbie. Now you know all about the little pest. That I can sic him on the little weirdie is the best part. They're both irritating so they suit each other. And now ... I do believe it's time for Sports Central on ESPN.

Logan

November 18
Jacqueline H.-M. *<antiarrhythmic, nasogastric tube>*
<u>11:00 a.m.</u>

Dear Ms. Zephyr,

Feeling much better today. I took the liberty of going back to change my signature from my November 12th journal entry. I must have still been under the effects of the medication after the fainting spell.

It was Remembrance Day on the 11th but I guess I didn't notice. In today's mail I received an interesting letter from my Nona. The two people I miss most in here are my dog Zoë and my Nona.

The letter was only a week late — not bad for Nona! She sent me a poppy. Not a real poppy — a plastic poppy. Nona was my age when World War II was on. She always says she has a soft spot for a man in uniform. Since you asked us to write our journal entry on the most influential person we know, I am working on the story of my Nona. I should have it completed by this afternoon, even though it is not due until tomorrow. This will be a first where my Nona is concerned. She is just about always late for everything. She says now that she's retired she'd rather have fun than always be on time.

And Abbie, I wonder if you could arrange for me to have my watch back?

Jacqueline (formerly known as Cleo)

November 18
Logan K.   *<corticosteroids>*
<u>Sometime after noon (With serious writer's cramp.)</u>

Okay, Abs, this is the last of the freakin' apology letters. Ten letters. Ten! I never knew there could be so many people in charge of one puny hospital. I had to borrow paper from your desk to write 'em, by the way.

I am never kicking anything in this place again. Too many consequences. Please tell me all this writing counts for my journal entry today. My hand looks like an owl's claw — I can't write any more.

L.

> **WHILE YOU WERE OUT**
>
> Abbie Z,
>
> Laptop computer dropped off at the front desk for your student Kip Graeme.
>
> We've locked it up for safekeeping. Just give us a call before you come down.
>
> Thx
>
> Karna, Reception

Journal Entry
November 18

My Favourite Influential Person: Sophia Clement-Jones
by Jacqueline Hornby-Moss

If asked the question about their favourite person of influence, many people would pick a famous movie star or political figure (and others would even pick some stupid rugby star that nobody has ever heard of), but I choose my grandmother. Her name is Sophia Clement-Jones and she is a very special and influential person.

Most grandmothers bake cookies, but mine doesn't. My grandmother lives in Clearwater these days, but she spent her whole career working as an astronomer in the Mount Wilson Observatory in California. Countless interesting things happened at that observatory. Famous astronomers like George Ellery Hale and Edwin Hubble made many discoveries using the Mount Wilson telescope. Of course, in those days women were not really allowed to call themselves astronomers (even though many were and my Nona was one of them).

Nona was working at the observatory when Walter Baade discovered the remnants of Keplar's supernova, which actually occurred way back in 1601. She says it was a very exciting time, seeing history so far in the past happen right before her eyes. Of course, she was only classified as an assistant then.

It wasn't until 1981 that the observatory hired its first woman telescope operator. I'm so proud my Nona was one of the first women who worked in astronomy. She didn't get her degree from university until she was sixty-two. But then they <u>had</u> to call her an astronomer. If my mother wasn't insisting I try out for the Miss Evergreen pageant, I would consider studying astronomy immediately after I finish high school. My sister plans to be a doctor if acting doesn't work out. My mother thinks that I should consider taking a stand for world peace, because it sounds better in pre-pageant interviews, but I would rather be an astronomer. Besides, all the contestants take a stand for world peace. But I digress.

Nona is also a very good grandmother. She always remembers my birthday (though usually a few days late) and she sends me letters all the time. When I was ten she gave me a puppy named Zoë. Zoë reminds me of Nona because they both have white hair and very bouncy personalities. I miss them both so much.

My Nona has a computer and knows how to send e-mail, too. After mastering that big telescope, she says no little computer is going to get the best of her.

What I appreciate most about Sophia is how she always finds time to spend with me. Even when everyone else is busy, she is always around. And when I am having a bad day, she says: "Cleopatra, just remember to be yourself and keep watching the stars." So I do.

by Jacqueline Hornby-Moss (but known to her Nona as Cleopatra)

6

Logan slammed the notebook down on the bed beside Kip.

"That's it! It's the essay Abbie made us write on the most influential person. Listen — she says it right here. 'Most grandmothers bake cookies, but mine doesn't. My grandmother lives in Clearwater these days, but she spent her whole career working as an astronomer in the Mount Wilson Observatory in California.'"

He closed the cover of the notebook with a snap.

"I think you've got it right, Kipper my boy. Cleo's gone to Clearwater."

Kip looked wide awake again. "Are you going to go get her tomorrow, Logan? Are you going to bring her back safe to the hospital?"

Logan's stomach clenched and the excitement of finding the clue he was looking for drained away. Cleo was hours ahead of him. Even if she was really only going to see her grandmother, he had a long way to go to find her. And if she was headed somewhere else — well, he couldn't even let himself think of that possibility.

"I think I'd better go now," he said quietly. "I'm pretty sure there's a bus I can catch that will get me there by morning. It's not a big town. I'll be able to find her, no problem at all."

Kip leaned forward and began pulling at the IV tape on the back of his hand.

"Whoa, hold on there, buddy. What do you think you're doing? If you bump that wire, you'll have the nurse back here in a flash, and that, my friend, will wreck everything."

"I want to come with you to find Cleo," said Kip, still peeling tape.

Logan reached over and pulled Kip's hand away. He took a deep breath to keep himself from yelling at the kid. "You can't come, Kip," he said, as calmly as he could. "If we want to find Cleo, I'm going to have to move like lightning."

He looked straight into the kid's eyes. "If you leave the hospital, you'll get really sick. You know that. But I can't do this without you. You can be my partner, okay?"

Kip's face brightened. "Your partner? Really?"

Logan nodded. "But we're going to have to work really fast, dude. We figure she's headed to Clearwater, right? So you can help me find her when I get there."

He grabbed Kip's laptop computer and flipped open the lid. Kip's face lit up with a reflected glow as Logan thrust the computer into his lap.

"First, we need to find out if I still have time to catch a bus before the station closes. Can you look up the bus schedule?"

Kip nodded and began tapping keys. Logan looked at his watch. "It's eleven thirty-five. Are there any more buses tonight?" He paced back and forth between the bed and the window.

"It says here that the last bus leaves Evergreen at midnight, Logan." Kip looked up from the screen. "Wow, that's really late."

"But does it go to Clearwater?"

"Uh," Kip ran his finger down the screen. "Yes! But it stops a whole bunch of places first."

"Okay, that's really good news." Logan stopped pacing and came to stand at the head of Kip's bed. "So here's the thing. My Blackberry is broken from the time I dropped it down the stairs, but I know there is an internet terminal at the bus station in Clearwater. My team went there last year for a rugby game. I think the café is called 'The Bean' or something."

Kip tapped the keys again. "It says here there is a 'Bean and Gone Café' at the Clearwater Bus Terminal with internet access."

"Yes!" Logan clenched a fist. "Soon as I get there, I'll send you an e-mail. And while I'm on the bus, you can look up any information you can find on Cleo's grandma. Between the two of us, we'll find her in no time."

"Okay," said Kip. "But maybe we should use instant messaging. It's faster."

"You're right, you're right. Okay, my e-mail address

is rugbyrox@yowza.com. 'Rugbyrox' is one word, and 'rox' is spelled with an 'x'. Got that?"

"Yeah, I got it. As soon as you e-mail me, I'll log into IM and we can talk on-line." He beamed, and Logan was suddenly glad he'd included the kid. He might actually end up being a help.

"Great. Okay, when I get there in the morning, I'll head over to the coffee shop and e-mail you. So just pretend to Abbie like you're doing homework and keep your e-mail connected, okay? That way if Cleo contacts you during the night, you can fill me in."

Kip nodded enthusiastically. "Are you going to put the notebook back on Abbie's desk?"

Logan shook his head. "Nah, I want to read through it some more. Maybe it has an address or something in the back. I'll have plenty of time. It's going to be a long bus ride." He looked at his watch again. 11:45 p.m. And it was a fifteen-minute run from the hospital to the bus station ... when he was in shape. "I gotta go, buddy. Watch for my e-mail, okay? It's really important. Just like 'M' in James Bond, right?"

"I remember him! He's in my computer game!"

Logan shook his head. What's wrong with kids these days? They spend so much time on this computer crap, you'd think they'd never heard of movies. "Geez kid — when I get back I've got a couple of shows you've gotta see, okay?"

"Really? Okay, Logan. Good luck." Kip was beaming,

and Logan found himself smiling back. But time was up. It was past up.

Logan tucked the notebook into the waistband of his scrubs and stuck his head out the door. A red light was flashing over the ICU wing and the three nurses were nowhere to be seen. Bonus! Time to hit the stairs running.

*   *   *

Logan's trip down the back staircase took place at a higher rate of speed than he had anticipated. His mind occupied by the conversation with Kip, he forgot his earlier meeting with the custodian. He never actually lost his footing, first sliding on the wet floor, then grabbing the handrail for support. And in a decision that took less than an instant, he thought that maybe riding the handrail down might prove to be the best course of action in any case. So he did.

He made it safely to the basement, had another close call when the custodian stepped unexpectedly out of the morgue (who expects anyone to step out of a morgue in the middle of the night, anyway?), and shot out the door with his coat in one hand and Abbie's notebook in the other. When he made it to the station there would be plenty of time to read through the notebook to find what he needed. He needed Cleo's grandmother's address. If it wasn't in the notebook, Kip might be able to find it. And as soon as he'd delivered what he had in his pocket to Cleo, he'd bring the notebook back to Abbie. She'd understand. She had to.

As he ran, he jammed his arms into the sleeves and took a moment to ensure the inner pocket was safely fastened before zipping the coat closed against the frigid night air. For cold it was — winter had well and truly come to Evergreen. In spite of his good intentions, Logan had to slow to a walk for a block or two when his insides twisted with pain from the unexpected running.

In direct contrast to the fire in his belly, his fingers and toes soon numbed in the sub-zero temperatures. His breath came in frozen gasps, the moisture crystallizing on his eyelashes and trimming the ends of the hair with white.

He jogged up to the bus station at 12:10 am. Ten minutes late. But in spite of all his anxiety, he found that he needn't have hurried after all. The engine block on the bus had frozen solid when the driver had stopped for a coffee and neglected to keep the vehicle running. In the end, Logan helped the driver clip the cables onto the battery and earned himself a free bus ride when the engine roared to life.

"Don't mention it to the ticket seller," the driver had muttered gruffly. "She's out for my job."

"I won't if you won't," said Logan, so grateful not to have missed his ride as to be feeling almost cheerful.

A woman was collecting money in a kettle to one side

of the station, having taken shelter from the storm. He had just watched the ticket seller sternly admonish her that there was to be no bell-ringing indoors. Logan ran over and stuffed his bus fare money into her collection kettle.

The non-bell-ringing woman wished him a happy holiday and promptly packed up her kettle. Logan and the last of her potential donors rolled away from the station at 12:30 a.m.

He settled back on the bus, one of only a handful of passengers to board on this late night journey. It was a milk run, scheduled to stop five or six times before the bus hit Clearwater. Logan leaned back into the musty seat to try to sleep. The seat smelled like old cigarettes and stale food and he couldn't find a way to get comfortable. His hand went to his inner coat pocket and he traced the shape of the object inside. It was no use. His stomach had settled down but sleep was still distant. The plastic bag holding the notebook was on the seat beside him, slipping from side to side as the bus shivered its way along the slush-rutted highway.

If he could somehow manage to find Cleo before everyone else, he wanted to tell her something that he'd finally figured out. Maybe it was just a question of listening to the right voices. Not the kind of voices that told a person to kick a hole in a wall or stuff your fingers down your throat. Other voices — other ideas. Maybe all heroes were not found on rugby pitches or prancing in front of the Hollywood paparazzi.

Then there was the question of the meds. She took these pills every day, right? He racked his memory. The hospital must have put them in the bottle for when Cleo was given the weekend pass. But he couldn't remember how often she took them or even what she needed them for. That she left them behind was the worst sign yet.

Logan rubbed his tired eyes. Who knew what he was going to say or do? He wasn't even sure himself. He just knew this journey might be worth something, if he could just find Cleo. He just needed to know she would be okay.

He stretched up and flipped on the tiny light above his head only to discover it was burned out. But the light over the next seat flickered on when he touched it, so he slipped in beside the window and opened Abbie's notebook. He could see the next notation was from Kip — something about happiness and chocolate cake. He remembered writing something for Abbie about happiness as well. What was it?

In the hospital, it was easy to forget how to be happy. That's the problem with happiness, isn't it? Just when you think you have it in your hand, it's gone and you're left with a fistful of air and nothing else. Logan tilted the notebook toward the light and began to read.

November 18

Kip G.　　*<immune suppressant>*

Did you see, Abbie? My mom brought in my laptop. Dr. Robbie said I could use it to do my school work so from now on I'm going to use it to type all my journal entries for you. My mom also brought me a printer cable, so at night when everyone in the office goes home, I can print off all my work.

Here is my journal entry for today:

My Laptop by Kip Graeme

My laptop is a great machine. I'm really happy because now I can play all my computer games instead of Xbox. Computer games are way better. My favourite is *Battlescene Historia*, because I get to replay all the great battles in history.

I also really like watching anime and drawing my own anime with a program on my laptop. This is why my laptop is so great. I showed it to Jacqueline and she said she liked it, too, and even showed me how to type her name. Logan didn't want to see my laptop, for some reason. Maybe tomorrow.

Also, Jacqueline doesn't have the tube thing hanging out of her nose anymore. They took it out today. That sentence wasn't about my laptop, but I still thought it was interesting and you said journals should be interesting.

From,
Kip

November 19

Kip. G.   *<immune suppressant>*

Hi Abbie,

Logan got mad at me this morning and I feel pretty sick today. That's all my news. But I know you like to read my journal, so I will write a little bit on what you asked.

What Makes Me Happy
by Kip, 6th Grade

Three things make me happy. Playing baseball with my dad is one. Eating my mama's chocolate cake is another. But the best is not being in the hospital. I don't have to stay for so long this time, do I? Is a week up yet?

From, Kip

November 19
Logan K.   *<corticosteroids>*
<u>Too early.</u>

Okay Abs, today you want me to write about something
that makes me truly happy. (Stupid assignment, by the
way. The little weirdie is going to force you to read all
about butterflies and moonbeams and crap like that,
y'know. And what would she know about Carl Sagan,
anyway? That chick is such a know-it-all.)
So, what makes me happy?
Beer.

Logan

November 19
Jacquie   H-M.   *<antiarrhythmic,   IV   nutritional
                    supplements>*
<u>1:00 p.m.</u>

Dear Ms. Zephyr,

This was to be a journal of celebration, as Medusa and
Dr. Valens have finally opened their eyes to the amazing
progress I am making in here and have withdrawn my
feeding tube. However, the joy of that event has been

quashed by something I have read in your notebook and I really feel I must protest.

As you know, over the weekend I submitted a ten-page essay on the subject you assigned: happiness and fulfillment. Ten pages. With footnotes! And when I return to check my mark in your notebook, not only is my essay (which I sincerely believe deserves an A+) <u>missing</u>, but I see by Logan's entry that he was allowed to submit nothing. Not even a single page! With the exception of the ridiculous paragraph he submitted earlier today, of course. I also notice that some time ago he was allowed (may I even say encouraged) to present some sort of comic strip as a substitute for a journal entry. I would not ever want to accuse you of favouritism, Ms. Zephyr (and certainly no teacher in their right mind would favour him over me) but I feel righteously indignant enough to share my concerns with you.

Please feel free to inform Mr. Logan Kemp that I prefer to be addressed as Ms. Hornby-Moss or even as Jacqueline. <u>NOT</u> Little Weirdie. It is true that I have relinquished my birth name, however the whole subject is none of his business and on top of that, his substitute is entirely unacceptable.

And while you are speaking to him, perhaps you might inform him that due to circumstances beyond my control, I have been forced to examine the night skies extensively in my life. As a result, I have developed a deep and profound interest in astronomy. I have read widely from the works of Carl Sagan and he was even friends with my Nona. And not once — NOT ONCE — did he ever say "I'm outta here." (He would never use such a vile contraction, I am quite sure.)

Back to my original point, Ms. Zephyr. I truly understand how little Kip is allowed such a brief entry. After all, he is only eleven years old and really is feeling poorly these days. But Logan is in tenth grade — a full year ahead of me. Justice has not been served here.

Jacqueline H-M.

November 19
Logan K.   *<corticosteroids>*
<u>Later.</u>

Abbie, be reasonable. Beer does make me happy. You should feel good that I'm not smoking dope. Half the team smokes, but those stupid idiots have no eye for the future. I want a scholarship to get me out of this puny town. Smoking dope makes a person too content to lie around in their own ~~shi~~ feces.

So how's that? Are you happy now?

Logan

November 19
Logan K.   *<corticosteroids>*
<u>Sometime after the overcooked spaghetti they tried to pass off as dinner.</u>

Sheesh, Abbie. This is not fair. You get to go home to your regular life and probably some kind of great dinner like pizza and I'm stuck here with the nurse from hell enforcing no TV until I make a third freakin' stab at this homework. Give me a break, Abbie — I even asked the little weirdie how to spell feces. You are one hard dudette, Abs. (Hard Abs — good one!)

But you hold all the power, so here goes:

<u>Happiness</u> by Logan Kemp

After giving this subject some deep thought, I have decided to write about rugby. Any fifteen-year-old guy in his right mind likes football, right? But the truth is that it takes a special type of guy to play rugby. Rugby is more physical than football. The players don't wear all the pansy padding that football players wear. We're only forced to wear helmets so the opposing team doesn't tear off our ears in the scrum.

It's faster and you need a strong, clear ability to communicate. My favourite part of the game is the scrum. This is where the forwards all work together, shoulder to shoulder, to try to gain control of the ball from the other team. Sometimes it feels like you are trying to make it down the field with the entire opposing team on your back.

You just don't see that kind of action in football.

I also like how after the game the whole team lies on the side of the field because we are too tired to move. We drink Gatorade and pretend it's beer. (Just pretend. Of course, I know that no kids in high school ever drink beer. We just don't like it. Right.)

And so, to make a clear concluding paragraph just like you asked, what makes me happy is playing rugby followed by not drinking beer.

I'm going to ask the nurse to call you and read this to you, so you can tell her to let me turn on the TV.

Logan

**Evergreen Hospital
Gift & Tuck Shoppe**

Attention: Ms. Abigail Zephyr,
            Hospital Educational Department Head
            Dr. Rob Valens, MD, DFM
            Children's Ward Nursing Staff

Please be advised that effective immediately, one of your patients, Logan Kemp, is not welcome in the Evergreen Hospital Gift & Tuck Shoppe until further notice. We have reason to believe that several incidents of shoplifting have occurred over the past two or three weeks. While we do not have security cameras, it is likely no coincidence that these stock losses have come during your patient's stay in hospital.

Though we have no actual proof that Mr. Kemp is involved, yesterday we set out a series of bait chocolate bars before his daily trip to "browse" through the store. The candy disappeared, but by the time our staff member had finished cleaning up an overturned fixture of rubber balls, Mr. Kemp had left the store and the bait candy was missing.

The proceeds from the Evergreen Hospital Gift & Tuck Shoppe are distributed to the Evergreen Knitters Guild, who knit woollen socks for needy children in Africa. These thefts constitute a loss to all who feel moved by the spirit of Christian charity.

Please inform Mr. Kemp that if he does try to return to the premises, he will be barred at the door.

I have owned and operated the Evergreen Hospital & Tuck Shoppe for twenty-seven years and have never experienced interaction with a patient displaying such moral depravity.

Thank you for your attention to this matter.

Sincerely,
Eusebes J. Pattison,
Owner and Operator,
Evergreen Hospital Gift & Tuck Shoppe

November 20
Logan K.   *<corticosteroids>*
<u>Some crappy morning time</u>

Today I feel like crap. The whole world is crap. And writing this journal entry every day is the biggest crap deal of all. I don't need English skills to be a rugby star. I just need someone around here to solve the problem of whatever is eating my gut out. Who was this Crohn guy, anyway? And why does he hate me so much?

I'm not really up to this journal stuff today.

By the way, I don't care that I've been kicked out of that crappy little store. Who needs them, anyway?

That little weirdie isn't helping. Okay, I give you that I shouldn't call the chick a weirdie. But there is no way I'm going to call her by some stupid, made-up name. And there's no denying she <u>is</u> weird. I mean, even before she broke her wrist she was trying to starve herself to death. And here's me who CAN'T eat because it kills my gut. It's just not freakin' fair. The truth is, that's why I kicked your wall in that time, Abbie. I was so mad at that chick. She could have a perfect life and she just chooses not to.

What kind of teacher keeps her notebook on the desk for anyone to read, anyway? I hate it when the weirdie looks at my stuff and then bugs me about it. Little Miss A Student is pretty quick to criticize other people. Maybe she should just keep her eyes on her own work and go eat a banana split or three. And have a look in the mirror while she's at it. Baby, she's got problems of her own.

I know Carl Sagan was an astronomer dude. I know he used to look at the stars a lot. The man must've said "I'm outta here" at some point in his life. And who gives a shit about Carl Sagan or what he said, anyhow? You can't see the stars from in here.

Logan

November 20
Jacqueline H-M.   *<antiarrhythmic, IV fluids>*
9:06 a.m.

Hello Abbie,

Well, there you have it. You have broken through my natural reserve. I have never called a teacher by her first name before. I have to admit it feels a little strange, even in writing.

But after our amazing discussion yesterday I just feel free to do as you have asked. I had no idea you were so interested and informed on the subject of astronomy. What a thrill for me to chat with such a knowledgeable resource! Plus, today is a day of celebration. First full day since Medusa finally removed my gastric tube, not that I needed the thing anyway. I feel quite sure I have turned a corner and am on my way to recovery.

Only nine days to my birthday — can you believe it? Abbie, I feel ready to become a whole new person. New name, new age, and new slim and attractive body. The NG tube removal means that I can start eating food again, and though I have some firm thoughts on the choices I must make, I am happy to get back to normal. You'll see on the wall of my room I have put together a collage of the world's most beautiful women, cut out of magazines from the waiting area. My art therapist suggested I make the collage to represent what I want in life and I am thrilled with the results.

I know I can never be as beautiful or as willowy as these women but I hope that even when I am old and grey I will always retain a certain sense of style.

Jaqueline H-M.

> **WHILE YOU WERE OUT**
>
> Abbie Z,
>
> Pls contact Jake Arnold,
> Phys Ed teacher at Ever-
> green High regarding
> Logan Kemp.
> Call 101-555-1212
> Thx
> Karna, Reception

November 20

Kip G.   *<immune suppressant>*

Hi Abbie,

Since I'm stuck in bed right now, Logan said it would be good if I asked you a favour. Is it okay for me to hook up to the internet from my room? Logan says he'll show me a couple of really cool games if I let him try to send an e-mail to his friend Tom. He keeps trying to reach Tom from the computer station at the end of the hall but Tom hasn't answered and Logan says that computer is screwed anyway. But Logan says teachers have special powers to get things done around here.

I send e-mails to my dad at work every day, and every night my mom sends me a goodnight e-mail before she goes to bed. But I usually don't get them until the next day because we are not supposed to use the internet station at the end of the hall at night time.

So can I?

From,
Kip

November 20
Logan K.   <*corticosteriods*>
<u>An ungodly hour in the morning.</u>

Okay, I get why you keep your notebook on your desk, all right? Everybody needs to look at it and you take away and file a bunch of the private stuff, anyway. I don't even care if the little weirdie reads my stuff. I just don't think she should be allowed to slag my work. It's one thing for her to be all stuck up about her English skills and her math skills and so on, but she should keep her opinions to herself. I mean, she has a lot to say for a girl who won't even use her own name because she thinks it's too boring. It's not boring. It's a good enough name. The one she made up is just plain stupid. A person who has something to say should have the backbone to use their own name. And she's so proud of her grandmother but won't use the name they share? Gimme a break. That chick is just too weird.

What really bugs me is she scoffed at my graphic novel. For your information, CLEOPATRA, it is <u>not</u> a comic strip. There's a difference, you know. Comic strips are like Garfield or Peanuts or something. And they can be pretty fun to read. But I happen to know <u>from my English teacher</u> that the graphic novel is a highly respected form of writing. And just because certain little weirdies can't draw worth spit is no reason for them to talk down about graphic novels. We read *Maus* in Grade 9 English and it was one of the best books I've ever seen. It was published in 1986, which was before a certain weird person was even born. And what about *The Sandman*? Neil Gaiman is a genius. Graphic novels rule.

So, even though I've written by far enough journal today, here's another panel of the novel, just because.

Logan Kemp, who always uses his real name.

As the sun heats the brackish water, is there a ripple to be seen where nothing has moved before?

Evergreen Hospital
Children's Ward – Desk 9
Office: 101-456-7890

November 21

To: Ms. Abigail Zephyr,
Evergreen Hospital Education Department Head

Re: Nutritional support for Cleopatra Jones

Dr. Valens has relayed a request from the hospital nutritionist that Cleopatra is required to resume a morning snack of protein bar/shake as her weight has not rebounded since the removal of the NG tube. Please ensure that Cleopatra be allowed a sufficient break from her morning studies to allow her time to take this important nutritional supplement. Please direct any questions to Dr. Valens. Thank you.

Takehiko Ken, RN

November 21
Kip G.   *<immune suppressant>*

Abbie, I showed Jacqueline my anime program today. She really liked it. She is so nice. I don't get why she changed her name, though. Logan says she is weird, but I think she is nice.

I feel sick.

Do I have to do my journal when I feel sick? Besides, Jacqueline and Logan are fighting over my laptop. They both want to send e-mails to their friends since the internet station at the end of the hall is broken. If I feel sick, do I have to do my math, Abbie?

From,
Kip

November 21
Jacquie H-M.   *<antiarrhythmic, IV fluids>*
<u>9:06 a.m.</u>

Hello Abbie,

I had a wonderful dinner with my mother and father last night and I wanted to tell you about it so you could see the progress I have made. After you left for the day my parents arrived with a pass from Dr. Valens so we could go out for a surprise dinner. We got to celebrate my sister Helena's successful win as second row dancer and understudy in a new play. They brought me a new skirt (size zero, can you believe it?) from the Gap to wear with my red sweater to dinner. My sister seemed not quite herself. She did say that she much preferred the understudy role to the main role itself as the director was really on the lookout for cows with big chests and she would not want to be considered one of those. My mother says for a special treat they will go to visit the plastic surgeon one more time as push-up bras are just not enough these days for a girl who has Hollywood in her sights. My dad read the paper since he doesn't like to comment on girl talk.

I want you to know, Abbie, that I ate my whole meal. My parents were so proud. They are convinced I will be ready to leave here soon, and much as I will miss you, Abbie, I am ready to go home.

I did get some bad news at dinner. My parents and I

had quite a long time to talk while my sister was in the restroom, and they told me that Nona has moved to a nursing home while I have been incarcerated. It seems she fell and broke her hip and needs extra care while she recovers. She sent me a gift, though: a beautiful little astrolabe from her collection. It's not the gold one, but it is quite old and valuable all the same. As you are so knowledgeable on the subject of astronomy, you must know what a precious gift this is to me. Mother and Daddy were quite worried that it would be stolen in the hospital but I assured them that I have a very safe place to keep it, and especially since Nona is not well I would like to have it near me.

I'm so thrilled you enjoyed my journal entry enough to send it off to my English teacher at school. Because of my parents' visit, I have been thinking so much about my dog Zoë and how happy I will be to see her when I get home at last. I thought you might appreciate reading all about Zoë and what she does every day. I hope Ms. Plato enjoys it, too!

With all the writing and math practice I have had here, returning to school is going to be a piece of cake. I feel totally ready to go back. And wait until that Adine Terrapini gets her eyes on my new skirt. I'm dying to see the look on her face.

Love,
Jacqueline

November 21
Logan K.   *<corticosteroids, reduced dosage>*
<u>Afternoon, thank god.</u>

So, Abs — did all my math this morning. Still working on the graphic novel, you'll be happy to hear. I'll have to show you my sketchbook because I'm not quite ready to hand you another finished panel. But I've got a problem.

Here's the thing. I know the chick is sick, all right? Mentally, I mean. But she's taken to puking in my washroom. MY washroom, Abbie. Now, let me tell you, my washroom is not a nice place. The cleaning staff just can't get in there often enough, and as you know, my own digestion is not exactly in order these days. But for some reason she seems to like it better than her own. I think she's hiding from the nurse and this is the second time in two days I've caught her. The first was the other night after she went out to dinner. I sure as hell don't understand this eating disorder thing. How can you go out for a great steak dinner and then want to stick your fingers down your throat?

I mean, cripes. At least she's got a normal family. A mom and a dad at home, still married with good jobs and all. A hot sister. Okay, I know that probably doesn't matter to the little weirdie but it still rules.

She even has a dog for crissakes. I would kill for a freakin' dog, man.

You know, I should be the one with the eating disorder, not her. Screwed up family, divorced dad living in Denver, works all the time, bonks his secretary and flies home for the odd weekend. Mother obsessed with charitable causes. Uh, how about looking a little closer to home, Angela? I can think of a half-decent charitable cause who lives in your son's bedroom upstairs.

Never mind. Forget I said anything. For all I know, my mom is off raising money to fight Crohn's disease across the country. The only thing more embarrassing than living with this stupid disease is having to be the poster child for your mother's charitable efforts.

Crap. I wish I hadn't thought of it. If you hear even a whisper that she is up to something, you'll tell me, right Abbie?

Logan

7

He flipped the notebook closed and dropped it on the next seat. The bus swayed back and forth in a hypnotic way. Probably everyone was asleep. He should be asleep, if he wanted to have any energy in the morning. Besides, it was weird to read through Abbie's notebook. It felt almost like his life was spilled out over these pages, all mixed in with Cleo's life and Kip's and everyone else who wandered in and out of their ward. He wondered how Abbie made sense of it all.

The bus lurched a little and Logan bumped his head against the window frame. He stared out into the darkness. What kind of fool's errand was this? Chasing some self-destructive teenage girl across who knows how many snow-crusted miles. He should be home in his bed, the way any other person with more than half a brain would be.

Cleo had called him at home before she ran away from the hospital, but he'd been out and hadn't heard her message on his machine until after dinner.

It felt like days ago, not just a few hours. He could still hear her voice, as clear in his memory as if she had been standing beside him.

"Logan, I'm going away. There's something important I have to do. I'm not going to tell you anything, and that way if anyone tries to ask you for information you won't be lying when you say you don't know. Thanks for helping me fake my way through that ward transfer form. It should buy me at least a day before everyone figures out where I'm going. I don't know where I'm headed after I do this one thing, but I'm pretty sure it won't be home. I'm not really in a position to ask you any favours, but since I probably won't be running into you anytime soon, I'm going to ask just one. If there's any way you can, stay in touch with Kip, will you? He might be a little kid, but he really looked up to you in the hospital and I bet even on the outside he could sure use a big brother figure like you. And since you're probably gagging already, I might as well tell you that I did hear what you said to me the other day. So you might not be a rugby star anymore. But you made a difference to me and to how I want to live my life. It may not be important to you, but it is to me."

And that was it. She hadn't even said goodbye.

He shivered a little and picked up the notebook again, her voice still echoing in his head. He'd done what she said. He'd been kind to Kip. Maybe now it was her turn to listen.

November 22
Jacqueline Hornby-Moss *<antiarrhythmic, IV fluids>*
<u>7:16 a.m.</u>

Dear Abbie,

Please feel free to show this entry to Mr. Kemp.

I most strongly protest Mr. Kemp's allegations that I have been using his washroom. It is all conjecture; he has never seen me in there. I have never been in there that I can recall. Yes, I felt a little ill after my dinner out with my family, but everyone around here gets so hysterical, I thought it better to keep it to myself. I wish he would do the same. You keep your nose out of my business, Logan Kemp.

Jacqueline

WHILE YOU WERE OUT

Abbie Z,
Pls call Cleopatra Jones' mother regarding missed counselling appt. Grandmother taken ill
101-555-1234
Thx
Karna, Reception

November 22
Jacquie H-M. *<antiarrhythmic, IV fluids, nutritional*
supplements>
10:14 a.m.

(Abbie, you'll be happy to know that I have had a chance to cool down somewhat from my earlier note to you. As usual, your advice is sound. Thank you for suggesting that I write this. I feel much better for having done so.)

Journal entry: A Plea to Logan

Dear Logan Kemp,

This morning after I read your note to Abbie I was very angry. I had a strong urge to wipe away your customary smirk with the swift blow of a bedpan to your face. Instead, however, I sat down and really tried to think through why you upset me so much.

I know more about you than you think I do. I know how much you love rugby. I know that you had a crush on Mary Margaret Johnston last year. (For your information, Mary Margaret herself told me about this, during Hip Hop Dance class after school. She seemed quite pleased about it, however, I believe you were wasting your time. In the end, she told me she prefers a more cerebral type. Sorry.)

I know how much you hate, loathe, and despise the disease that has attacked you. And I know how much your stomach hurts. I've seen you running to the bathroom.

But you don't know anything about me. And that's my problem.

I'm pretty sure you don't care, either. But on the slim chance you do, here's a newsflash.

My stomach hurts, too. It hurts every time I look at food. If I have to eat something, it starts to hurt from the time I even smell the food. It hurts going down. It hurts when it hits my stomach. And yes, it hurts when I bring it back up again. (Except this last bit has so much relief involved it makes the hurt seem less, for some reason.)

I know that food is fuel. I understand that my behaviour is destructive. I can see that my health might be affected someday. But it still hurts.

Some pain is worth the price. I get that. I've seen you steal chocolate from the gift shop downstairs. And just so you know, I've kept a running tally. I've counted seven candy bars, which means you've probably stolen at least double that. You are most certainly what my father refers to as a slippery character and how you can steal from those sweet old people I do not know. It was no surprise to me when they banned you from the premises. And I'm not even going to attempt to address the question of why you steal in the first place when you have so much money of your own. Who knows what makes you do these things?

Remember that time we were doing math and you were sneaking raisinettes? I said you'd be sick. And I was right. I've never seen anyone attached to an IV pole run as fast as you did to the rest room. But you know what? Other people hurt, too. And I am a <u>person</u>, not a weirdie.

You take medicine to get better or at least to help with your pain. I do too, but it doesn't work. And that art therapist with her huge glasses and wild theories gives me no help at all. The only thing that actually makes me feel better is talking with Abbie. I want to spend my time doing that and NOT putting so much energy into ignoring your mean remarks. So cut it out, will you? I deserve that much, I think.

Jacqueline

November 22
Logan K.   <*corticosteroids, minimal dosage*>
<u>Before noon, can you dig it?</u>

Hey Abs,

You in some kind of meeting? I can't find you anywhere. So don't have a stroke, but I've got all my work done for the day. Beat the lunchtime rush, that's my rule. Journal, math, even that science write-up that Mr. Shima sent from school. Not bad if I do say so myself.

I walked by Kip's room earlier. Sleeping in, the little slacker. Trying to get out of homework is my guess. Maybe I'll go give him a hand so I can use his laptop when he's done. Still haven't heard back from the team about the tryout dates. My gut is almost back to normal. I'm sure I'll be ready to try out whenever they need me.

Later!
Logan

Evergreen Hospital
ICU Ward – Desk 11
Office: 101-456-7890

November 22

To: Ward Nurses – Children's Ward, Desk 9
Re: patient Kip Graeme

Please note that this patient has been formally transferred out of the Children's Ward and into ICU. Tutoring is cancelled until further notice.

cc Dr. Rob Valens, MD, DFM
cc Ms. Abigail Zephyr,
    Education Department Head

November 25
Jacqueline   H-M.   *<antiarrhythmic,   IV   fluids,*
nutritional supplements>
<u>9:11 a.m.</u>

Good morning, Abbie. Hope you had a great weekend.

Actually, the truth is that this isn't really a very good morning at all. You missed a lot when you were away visiting your family. As you probably know by now, poor little Kip was rushed to surgery after he rejected his kidney. His mom sat crying on my bed for hours on Saturday, but by Sunday he was doing pretty well. He has to be hooked to a machine for regular dialysis every day, since he no longer has even a single working kidney to clean out his blood.

But now that Kip is feeling better, I am trying to find something to feel thankful about. Today is one month until Christmas and four days until my birthday — both exciting. Maybe soon I'll be back at school. I'm hoping Adine has been eating way too much and by the time I get back to school she'll look like a little pink pig with an apple in her mouth.

I'm going to think more about this thankfulness essay before I write it, Abbie. Will have it to you before deadline, though, for sure.

Jacqueline

From the Desk of Donna-Fay Jones

Dear Ms. Zephyr,

A brief note to say that we will not be over as usual to visit Cleopatra this week. Her grandmother is doing poorly and we have had to spend some extra time in Clearwater as a result. We should be back by the end of the week.

Sincerely,
Donna-Fay Jones

November 25
Jacquie H-M. *<antiarrhythmic, IV fluids, increased nutritional supplements>*
<u>11:36 a.m.</u>

I'm back, Abbie. And I've thought about being thankful. But I have to say that thankfulness just isn't my cup of tea today. I am thankful that Kip is better and all that, but I mean, let's get real for a minute. Sometimes (and I can't believe I'm saying this) Logan is right. Look around you. If you were a kid having to live in the hospital, how thankful would YOU be?

Remember the history assignment you gave Logan and me last week about the rise of communism in Europe? I don't know if he even read the pages you gave us — I did see him sleeping in the lounge with a copy on his face, so maybe he did. But I read it, Abbie and it's made me think. Marx and Engels put a few words down on paper and they pretty much changed the shape of history forever. And today when Medusa was taking my blood pressure for the four hundredth time I decided that now is the time for me to take action.

The Communist Manifesto basically outlined Marx's idea that if people work as hard as they are able and take only what they need, then society can run without the need for wealth or poverty. It was a pretty good idea when you think about it, but it seems that there has been some trouble ever getting it to work properly.

We don't really have a problem with wealth and poverty here in the hospital, but we do have some other BIG problems. I've decided the answer to our problems is a Sick Kids' Manifesto. I have an enthusiastic supporter in Kip, who agrees with me wholeheartedly. Now, if I can only get Logan to pay attention we might all benefit.

So far, this is what I have:

EVERGREEN HOSPITAL
SICK KIDS' MANIFESTO

A spectre is haunting this hospital. The spectre of totalitarianism. Too many nurses and doctors are taking too much power over the proletarian patients. And the parental bourgeoisie just look the other way.

We, the Proletarian patients, DEMAND ACTION.

Okay, so that's what I have so far, Abbie. I'm not quite sure what action we will actually demand. For myself, I would prefer a little <u>in</u>action for a change. Less interference in my personal space. But action will be taken — I guarantee it. I just need to think it through a little more.

Oh, and by the way, one of the things I AM thankful for is that you are willing to listen to me. That weird art therapist is always wanting me to embrace my inner child or admit to some terrible family secret. I'm trying

124

to grow up here, Abbie, not revisit my inner child. And my worst family secret is that my mother didn't make it as a movie star when she moved to California in her youth. Pretty bad, huh?

Jacqueline

November 25
Logan K.   *<corticosteroids, minimal dosage>*
Before noon.

Why I am Thankful by Logan Kemp

I am thankful because my gut is improving and a couple of days ago the doctors even started using the word remission. I didn't even know what remission meant until today — always thought it had something to do with cancer, I guess.

I am really thankful that it looks like I'll be able to come off the IV line (aka the Useless Contraption) pretty soon. The nurses have already given me a few hours off it here and there. But being off Useless will mean I am one step closer to getting out of here and back onto the rugby pitch. (We play even if it snows. You've gotta be tough to play rugby.)

I am thankful that the little kidney kid is okay, too, though he is still pretty sick. The nurses might seem tough around here but, let me tell you, they are totally harsh in ICU. I couldn't even sneak in to give the kid a few Skittles. Still, I managed to wave the bag at him through the window as an incentive to get better. I'm sure he saw me.

Weird Cleopatra was on my case about the Skittles, too. She ranted at me for five minutes about not offering Kip temptation. What's life without a little temptation, for crissakes? Personally, I think she wanted them for herself.

Okay, I know this piece is supposed to be about thankfulness, so here's a good one for you, Abbie. I am thankful I am not as weird as Cleopatra.

I thought she was weird before, but this is the worst. Yesterday when I was finally allowed to unplug from Useless for an hour, I went out to the courtyard. You know it, right? It's not really enclosed, more like a letter C. Anyway, when I got down there I stretched out on a bench in the sun to catch a few rays. (Lucky I did, because it looks like snow out there today.) Anyway, after a few minutes I heard something so I opened my eyes and who do you think was down there skulking about? Weird Cleopatra was creeping along, face practically on the ground, pockets stuffed with plastic bags. How she even managed to get out of the ward is a mystery to me.

I was lying on the back of the bench facing the other wall so she didn't notice me watching her through a slit in the bench. Abbie, the chick was picking up dog crap. Yeah, you read that right.

Okay, I know she's got control issues but what kind of neat freak cleans up the hospital grounds after the local dogs? I think she's got a new obsession with dogs. Did you see that journal entry the other day? Ten pages about her stupid dog. I love dogs, but ten pages? I hated that dog by the end. (Oh, and by the way, I figure you must have hated it, too, since I notice her little dog essay has disappeared from your notebook. Way to go, Abs!)

So, to wrap up, I am thankful that one day when I get a dog it will not be as weird as Cleopatra's dog.

Logan

WHILE YOU WERE OUT

Patient Logan Kemp, Ward 9, Rm 307

Please call Jake Arnold, Phys Ed teacher, Evergreen High.
Re: Rugby tryouts
101-555-1234,
Thx
Karna, Reception

November 25
Logan K.   *<corticosteroids, minimal dosage>*
<u>Sometime on a crappy snowy afternoon.</u>

Just so you know, Abbie, cancel all the stuff I said I was thankful for. I am thankful for nothing. Evergreen High School stinks and the rugby team stinks and the biggest stink of all comes from a coach who would stab one of his most focussed players in the back.

I'm going to bed.

Logan

8

This had to be the stupidest idea he'd ever had. Reading his own words on paper made Logan feel sick. He hadn't known — really known — how hard it was for Cleo back then. Even the note to Abbie from Cleo's teacher showed things were bad. But she wasn't the only one with problems.

The loss of his position on the rugby team still felt like a physical blow. Logan took a deep breath as the bus lurched forward after yet another stop. He turned his breath against the glass of the window but the cold still defeated him. Sometimes, no matter how hard you try, you just can't win.

A few stops back he'd held his palm to the window until the feeling had completely left his fingers, but in the second or two before the window frosted over his palm print, he had still been unable to see any kind of place sign or landmark. Clearwater was the last stop on the night's run, so there was no danger Logan would fall asleep and miss it. And stupid idea or not, Cleo was out there somewhere. There had to be a way to make things right.

November 26
Jacqueline H-M. *<antiarrhythmic, IV nutritional supplements>*

Abbie,

I wonder if you can please send the attached note through by e-mail to my mother. The internet down the hall is broken again and of course I can't borrow Kip's computer anymore.

Thank you for your help, Abbie.

Jacqueline

Hello Mother,

When you get a moment, could you please call me at the hospital? I've tried you several times but it always flips to your voice mail and the box is FULL. I am anxious to hear about how Nona is doing. She hasn't sent me any letters or cards for two weeks at least. And I wanted to tell her how well I did on the essay I wrote about her.

Your daughter,
Cleopatra

Evergreen Hospital
ICU Ward – Desk 11
Office: 101-456-7890

November 26

To: Ward Nurses – Children's Ward, Desk 9

Re: patient Kip Graeme

Please note that patient transfer has been completed from the Intensive Care Unit to the Children's Ward.

cc Dr. Rob Valens, MD, DFM
cc Ms. Abigail Zephyr,
   Education Department Head

November 27
Kip Graeme   *<analgesic, anticoagulant, EPO,*
                                phosphate binder>

(I can't believe I got talked into this. This better give me some kind of good Samaritan points, Abbie. L.K.)

Hi Abbie,

This is Kip. Logan said he would type for me since I feel so crummy and I can't sit up yet. But I wanted to tell you that I am happy to be back here in this ward. I even got Logan's bed! They moved him into my room so I could be with you during the day. I like sharing a room with you, Abbie!

(Hey — I like the privacy. He's all yours, Abbie. L.K.)

Logan, no typing what I am not saying. What are you typing now? Cut it out.

(Okay, okay, kid. Just joking around. L.K.)

Abbie, I am so sad that my donated kidney didn't work. But maybe I will get another new kidney soon. My mom says I am on the list to try again so that I don't have to be hooked up to this machine for life. It is called d____s .

(No way I can spell that, Abs. You know what the kid means, right? The kidney cleaner thing. L.K.)

Logan has been really cool. He drew all these

amazing cartoon pictures of cars that I have all over my walls now. Thanks, Logan!

(This is really stupid, Abs. I'm only writing this because he said it. And I didn't twist the kid's arm or anything, if that's what you're thinking. And they are NOT cartoons, kid. Illustrations. They are illustrations.)

He also told me how he is teaching himself to drive by using his mom's car when she is asleep.

(Okay, now that's privileged information, Abbie. You can't divulge that by law, right?)

Thanks for typing for me, Logan. Doctor Robbie says I can sit up tomorrow, so I will type my own then.

From,
Kip

November 27
Logan K.   *<IV shunt withdrawn>*
<u>Afternoon.</u>

Thanks for taking my scribing job for Kip as my journal entry for the day, Abs. You rock!

And I am now finally free of the Useless Contraption. The nurse just removed my IV shunt. Bonus!

Logan

November 27
Jacqueline H-M.   *<antiarrhythmic, IV nutrition>*

Hello Abbie,

I just reviewed the segment Logan typed out for
Kip. Thank you for confirming that the contents of
this notebook are confidential. I certainly would not
want any of the following information getting out.

I just had a very disturbing telephone call from my
sister. It seems she was invited to a party held by a group
of sorority sisters at the state college. My sister was thrilled
to be invited but was very perturbed when she arrived and
found a number of girls my age were also in attendance.
Including the one and only Adine Terrapini. It seems
Adine's sister (one of the sorority girls) gave each of the
younger girls a different coloured lipstick before they
opened the doors and displayed a room full of fraternity
boys who had obviously been invited earlier. Helena told
me that the girls were invited to a rainbow party. All the
girls had on bright colours of clothing but I don't think
they really understood what was going on, Abbie. Helena
said she and a bunch of the other girls left as soon as
it became clear where the rainbows were supposed to
show up. But she said Adine stayed behind, laughing and
drinking Jack Daniels with the fraternity boys.

This makes me feel quite sick. I'm so glad Helena
left the party. I even — and I can't believe I am

writing this — wish Adine had left, too. (Apparently Helena kept the lipstick, though. She said it was a very pretty coral colour.)

Jacqueline

November 28
Kip G. *<analgesic, anticoagulant, EPO, phosphate binder>*

Hi Abbie,

Okay, this is really funny, Abbie. Logan just told me that Jacqueline just got caught putting dog poop in her toilet. For some reason Logan looked really upset, but I think it is a pretty funny joke to play on the nurses. Jacqueline is always mad at the nurses. She says she has no privacy. I just hope they know she was joking. It is a pretty funny joke, don't you think, Abbie? She won't get in trouble, will she?

I can see Jacqueline through the window to Logan's room, but the door is closed and I can hear him shouting. He must be mad about something because he is banging stuff around in there again. I guess we can laugh about this later.

From,
Kip

November 28
Logan K.
<u>After cooling down some — afternoon, I think.</u>

Hey Abs,

You may have already heard from Cleopatra about our little dust-up this morning. I just blew a gasket, Abbie. I mean, I did read the note she wrote to me. I do get that she's battling something that I don't really understand and I am really trying not to bug her about it.

But I've been thinking about this. It seems to me the biggest dragon she has to slay is herself. And when I found those laxative wrappers stuffed into my garbage can today ... well, I just lost it. You know I'm not commonly a garbage picker, but today Kip wanted to see what the rough copy of the latest panel of my graphic novel looked like, so I went back through the old pages I had just thrown away. And there were the wrappers, in with all the paper recycling. And I sure as hell knew that I haven't been eating chocolate laxatives.

What really bugged me is that she denied it. I guess I shouldn't have been surprised. I mean, she's denied barfing in my bathroom. She's had heart problems right from the time she got here and denies those, too. But lying to my face that she put the wrappers in my garbage? Well, anyway, it wasn't a good scene.

I don't know if she heard anything I said. She did

admit doing it, in the end, but she was crying pretty hard. Abbie, I honestly didn't want her to cry, just to come clean that she had been lying to me. I guess I didn't realize until we had the fight that she had also been lying to herself. I tried to tell her that she is worth something, and she shouldn't just throw her life away. Apparently she's been trying to reach her mother, but the woman has been too busy to see her own daughter, for some reason. Parents can really screw you around sometimes. I should know. My dad hasn't actually found time to speak to me in months. And Cleo does have someone on her side. I mean, the chick's mother might be an idiot but at least her grandmother loves her.

Anyway, when she got mad she threw something at me. If she comes to talk to you, maybe you can tell her I have it.

I guess the good thing is that I didn't kick any walls in this time.

Logan

November 28
Kip G. *<analgesic anticoagulant, EPO, phosphate binder>*

Hi Abbie,

It's just me again. Kip. I can't find you and I need to tell you something important. Logan is gone. Dr. Valens

137

stopped by and signed him out this afternoon and his mom came and picked him up. It was so sudden! I think he was surprised. He came in and gave me all his car drawings. They are not cartoons, Abbie. This is Very Important to remember. His mom was all dressed up when she came to get him, but I don't think he wanted to get dressed up, too. I thought he might be happier to go home, but he looked a bit sad. He couldn't find you or Jacqueline to say goodbye to. I pretended I was you and gave him a hug and he pretended to be mad but I know he wasn't really.

I'm sad he's gone. Do you think he'll come to visit me?

From,
Kip

November 28
Cleopatra Jones   *<antiarrhythmic, oral>*
<u>11:56 p.m.</u>

Abbie, I don't really know what to say. But whatever I say, I want to do it now — before my birthday actually gets here. I'm so sorry I let you down. And I'm even sorry I called Logan a snivelling, sneaking, spying slime, too. I was going to apologize to him in person when we'd both cooled down a bit, but then

Kip told me he had been discharged. He'll probably never come back here again. I wouldn't if I was him.

It was so nice of you to stay late tonight to make time to talk with me. You were right. Stooping to collecting ... you know what ... was a sign that things have gotten a bit out of control.

But you have no idea how gross these nurses can be. I mean, I've been here for almost a month now and I've gotten pretty used to Medusa and her moods. I'm not sure I believe you when you say they want the best for me. Well, I guess I <u>do</u> know they want the best, but they don't always find the nicest way to go about it. I knew they were monitoring my food intake once they took out the naso-gastric feeding tube. I just didn't know they kept track of my food output, too.

So thank you for speaking up for me. I truly won't put any more dog poop in the toilet, I swear. It's too disgusting to collect, anyway. I just wanted to pay Medusa back for doing something so dehumanizing and personally embarrassing to me. I know it was wrong. I even knew it at the time. I know she really wants the best for me and I'm not the easiest patient in the world. And writing the Sick Kids' Manifesto got me thinking about taking power into my own hands. So when I got the idea, I just couldn't resist.

I know, I know. It was a really stupid idea. And now I AM sorry.

Not only that, Abbie, but I am going to get better. Really. I've put my mind to it, and you know what a good mind I have! I realize now that this was not behaviour befitting anyone named Jacqueline Hornby-Moss. Which brings me to my last point.

I can't believe I am actually writing this, but Logan was right about one thing. ONLY one thing, but still.

I AM proud of my Nona. And I am proud of my name. My mother named me for one of the most beautiful women who has ever lived. I know I will never be able to live up to it. But no more Jacqueline Hornby-Moss. It's reality time, and you helped me see that. (I guess Logan did, too.) So thank you.

Cleo

November 29
Kip G. *<analgesic, anticoagulant, EPO, phosphate binder>*

Hi Abbie,

My dad is going to give me his kidney. He says that he had some tests done after my other kidney stopped working and the day before yesterday they came through as A-O-K. My mama didn't want me to worry so they saved the surprise for today. It's

Cleopatra's birthday and I get a new kidney all in one day! Jacqueline says that I should call her Cleo now, and that Jacqueline was just a dumb made-up name she has outgrown now that she is fourteen. (I like Cleo better, anyway. It's easier.)

I have to go now. I'm a little scared but not very. My dad will be in the operating room next to mine. I will see you soon, Abbie.

Love,
Kip

Evergreen Hospital
ICU Ward – Desk 11
Office: 101-456-7890

November 29

To: Ward Nurses – Children's Ward, Desk 9

Re: patient Kip Graeme

Patient Transfer – Surgery followed by ICU.
Kidney transplant.

cc Dr. Rob Valens, MD, DFM
cc Ms. Abigail Zephyr,
    Education Department Head

November 29
Cleo J.   *<antiarrhythmic, oral>*
<u>7:03 p.m.</u>

Happy Birthday to me.

Friday night. Perfect night for a party. Except no one remembered. You didn't come into work today, Abbie. I know you're not allowed to come in here if you have a cold and I guess you are entitled to a sick day now and again. But on my birthday?

My sister is gearing up because Miss Winter Snowflake has laryngitis and now my sister gets her moment in the spotlight. I know my mom is going crazy sewing Helena's new baton-twirling costume. And she has to worry about calling the nursing home about my grandmother. Nona is not doing well. My mother sent me flowers for my birthday, which did not make things easier, especially since she couldn't find the time to come herself. I know she meant well, but I was pretty upset when they arrived.

Flowers are for dead people and I truly fear Nona will soon be one of them.

It's probably just as well that no one was here for my birthday. The day has certainly not turned out as I had hoped. I'm now fourteen years old and, according to Medusa, I've gained seven pounds. She says I'm now eligible to go home for a weekend whenever I want. How fun — home to an empty house for a weekend, with no clothes to wear because I am too fat for everything. Seven pounds means saying sayonara to my new Gap skirt. I can still get it done up but all you can see is bulging stomach. Maybe if I put my big red sweater over it I could get away with it if I do go home. If I plan it right, I can walk through the mall when Adine Terrapini is hanging out with her hoodlum friends. "Hi Adine! Notice my size-zero skirt from the Gap?"

And she'd say ... nothing. Just look right through me and chew gum like a cow. Maybe with a vapid giggle or two. At my expense, of course. "Heh-heh. Hey Eddie. Look at the fat kid, trying to pull off a size-zero skirt. Who does she think she is ... a hippo in a bikini?"

To give credit where it is due, Logan remembered my birthday. He actually choked down his hatred of the hospital for an hour and came back to the ward to bring me a gift. But in the end, it didn't go very well. Before the flowers came I did get a chance to say sorry about

143

our fight yesterday, but he was feeling sort of down, himself. He thinks his dad will be mad at him. It seems he missed the tryouts after all. Anyway, he's not on the rugby team and he's pretty bummed. Guess that makes two of us.

Cleo

Sent: November 30
To: a_zephyr@evergreen.org
From: RugbyRox@yowza.com

Hey Abbie,

You've probably read the report by now, but Dr. Valens says that he thinks I can be pretty much treated as an outpatient from here on in. Wish I felt more like celebrating.

I know it's your day off and all, but I want to let you know that Cleo is feeling pretty low and I'm worried she's going to do something stupid. I mean, she's already done many stupid things but I just don't want it to get worse.

Now that I'm out, I'm hoping she'll be out soon,

too. Fellow sufferers, y'know — that's all. Don't read anything into it. We've kinda been through a few things together, so I'd like to see her do okay.

Anyway, I was feeling bad about the whole rugby disaster and I couldn't face hanging out at school. So since it was her birthday and all I dropped by to bring her a celebration chocolate bar now that she's eating once in a while.

Turns out the nurse had just told her she'd gained weight — a good thing, if you ask me — but Cleo was upset. Takehiko said she can go out on day passes any time now. But her family didn't show up for her birthday and of course she had to spend it in the hospital. So she was pretty low, but she ate the chocolate bar anyway, which I thought was a good sign.

Things sorta took a turn for the worse when the flowers arrived from her mom. I don't know what kind they were, but man, was she pissed. The card said: "Sorry we missed your birthday, sure you'll understand." Cleo did NOT understand. She ripped the head off every single flower and then gave the dead stems back to the poor delivery guy and told him to take them away.

Then she went into my bathroom, didn't even close the door, and barfed up the chocolate bar. I would have been totally grossed out if I hadn't been so sad for her. I thought she was getting better. She was still crying when I left.

Maybe you can think of something. I can't.

Logan

Evergreen Hospital
ICU Ward – Desk 11
Office: 101-456-7890

November 29

To: Ward Nurses – Children's Ward, Desk 9
Re: patient Kip Graeme

Patient Transfer – ICU to Children's Ward
Patient stable. Kidney transplant successful. Expect transfer to Children's Ward November 30.

cc Dr. Rob Valens, MD, DFM
cc Ms. Abigail Zephyr,
    Education Department Head

WHILE YOU WERE OUT

Message for patient Kip Graeme, Ward 9, Rm 307

Dictated message from 'Cleo': "Remember our talk. Promises are important!"

Did not leave return #.
Thx
Karna, Reception

To: a_zephyr@evergreen.org
From: JH-M@coldlist.com

Abbie, by now you have probably figured out that I have not been transferred to a different ward. I don't care what the other staff think, but I know that you are a good person and have always wished the best for me. I want you to know that I am never returning to that hospital hell-hole. I have endured one humiliation after another. It is simply more than a person can bear. You are the only good thing about the place (well, little Kip is pretty special, too) and therefore I want you (and Kip and Logan) to know that I am safe and you don't have to worry about me at all.

I did want to take this chance to say …

9

The bus lurched violently sideways and Logan jerked awake. He could hear a babble of voices, but there was nothing to be seen in the black night. Even his little nightlight overhead had gone out. He looked around blearily for a moment and then, grateful for the darkness, wiped the side of his face where he'd drooled onto the smelly seat.

With a blast of cold air, the bus driver climbed back onto the bus. *Where's he been?* thought Logan, still foggy.

"Sorry, folks. End of the line. That last rut took us straight into the ditch and nothing short of a tow truck is going to get us out of here tonight."

The driver cut off the chorus of groans with the wave of a hand. "Don't fret! We're only two city blocks from the bus station. For those of you who aren't interested in making the trek, another transport will be along smartly to ferry you to the station. Otherwise, it's only a short clip. And I'll turn the engine back on to keep you warm."

Logan realized he must have been more tired than he thought. He didn't remember falling asleep, but here he was at the end of the line. As the engine revved to life, the light came on over Logan's seat again. He ignored the grumbling of the other passengers and gathered up the pages of Abbie's notebook that lay scattered at his feet. A bit damp, some of them, but he thought he had them all. Somehow, though, the last page he'd been reading was torn. Maybe he'd ripped it in his sleep? He dropped to his knees and peered under the seat. Nothing.

He stuffed all the loose pages into the notebook and slipped the whole thing into the plastic bag. Logan pulled himself to his feet and clomped down the centre aisle of the bus. The driver nodded at him and Logan stepped out into the frigid night, immediately regretting his decision. He ducked his head further into his hood and pointed himself in the direction of the lights that blinked "*Pus Sta ion*" a block and a half away.

*   *   *

Three a.m. A bad time of the morning for feeling cheerful and worse when a person's fingers are so frozen they couldn't dial a phone for help even if there was a phone to dial. Logan slogged up to the bus station just in time to see the other bus passengers pull up in a heated cab with luggage stowed in the open trunk. The adversity of the weather must have had some kind of bonding effect as there was much hugging and bellowing of good-byes in the frozen air before they all headed off into the icy dark. The coffee shop was closed and as Logan crunched across the ice to the main door of the station a man inside flipped off the remaining lights and stepped out into the cold.

"We're shut down for the night, young fella," he said briskly.

"But I don't have anywhere to stay until daylight," said Logan. "I thought this was an all-night coffee shop."

"In Clearwater?" The man laughed. "Best head for the Sally Ann, young man. They can usually find a bed for homeless folks. Might be a little tight for space on a night this cold, though."

Homeless? Logan opened his mouth to tell the guy he wasn't homeless, but his audience was walking away. The man waved at the bus driver, who was stepping into a waiting car. The car honked twice — two sharp staccato notes that cut through the air like crystal. The man turned back to look at Logan. "I've got to go, young fella. Burt's missus was kind enough to offer me a lift. She doesn't like driving on icy nights, so I can't keep her waiting."

He pointed across the street and down a few blocks, in the direction the bus had just come from. "The shelter's back there, maybe a block before where the bus conked out. No walk at all for a strapping young man like yourself. You'll be there in no time." He climbed into the waiting car, which gave another sharp honk and then pulled away, red taillights gleaming like a wolf's eyes in the darkness.

Logan huddled in the bus station doorway and looked out across the street. Clearwater's downtown had seen better days. There were at least a dozen cars abandoned to either cold or rust along the main road. Many of the storefronts were shut down with windows boarded over. Logan kicked at a chunk of frozen muck on the sidewalk in frustration. He was not anxious to make the return trip across the same icy, rutted road he had already struggled along once that evening.

His head snapped up to the sound of footsteps crunching through the frozen snow. A figure seemed to materialize out of the shadows into the pool of light beneath the only streetlamp that still functioned outside the station. His breath formed a cloud around his head and he looked at Logan through one good eye. The other appeared to be swollen shut. His feet were encased in old rubber boots tied up inside clear plastic grocery bags. "Cold enough fer ya?" he asked cheerfully.

What am I supposed to say to that? thought Logan. *Is this guy crazy?* He finally settled on "Yeah. I guess so."

"Plannin' on standing out here all night? Station's closed, y'know."

"Uh, yeah. I do know." Logan wasn't about to tell this old idiot anything about what he was planning.

"Well, yer welcome to keep company with me. I'm headin' back to the highway. Need to hitch a ride to Evergreen. It's too damn cold in this fool town."

Logan was shocked out of his speechlessness. "I've just come from Evergreen," he said. "I'm not going back there. The guy from the station told me about the Salvation Army shelter ..."

"Full up, son. Jest been there m'self, I'm sorry to say. No room at the inn and all that. You come with me. Buddy o' mine's got a place in Evergreen we can crash at. Be there by morning. When it's this cold, no problem catching a ride. People feel sorry for ya freezin' on the side of the freeway."

"I can't. I need to stay here in Clearwater. I ... I'm meeting someone here in the morning."

"Suit yerself. It'll be a cold wait out here, though yer young bones likely don't feel it the way mine do."

Right, thought Logan, bitterly. *I hadn't even noticed the cold*. He shrugged and turned away.

The old fellow put a hand on Logan's arm. "If yer set in yer mind, then you might have a look at that shop over there. See the one with the plastic on the window?"

Logan repressed a desire to yank his arm out of the man's grasp. He peered through the darkness across the street where something was flapping in the wind. He nodded. "I see it."

"One of them boards at the front is loose," said the old guy, tucking his head down away from the wind. "There's a burning barrel inside to keep ya warm, but better make sure you damp the flames down good before dawn. Cops around this town ain't too friendly towards strangers." He winked his good eye at Logan, nodded, and was gone into the darkness before Logan could think of any reply.

"Thanks," Logan yelled, but the wind whipped the word back into his face. He hurried across the road to see if what the old drifter had said was true. Sure enough, under a sign saying "DAYAL'S MARKET," Logan found a board that was loose. He pulled it as far away from the door frame as he could and squeezed through.

Just being out of the gale made him feel as though he had stepped into a warm cave. The store smelled as though something had rotted very thoroughly somewhere inside, but Logan was still overcome with a wave of relief. He hadn't realized how anxious he really had been. Stepping cautiously in the dark, Logan clanged one of his boots into something large and metal. The ashy smell told him he'd found the burning barrel. He spent a few minutes scrambling around to pick up a pile of debris from the floor but realized how foolish this was just as he stuffed the material into the barrel. No matches. No lighter. The thing was useless to him.

His eyes adjusted to the dark, and a little warmer from all the exercise, Logan stepped toward the outline of something low a few feet away. It turned out to be an old wooden bench. Logan sank down on the bench and pulled out Abbie's notebook from his pocket. He could feel moisture on his cheeks from his hair and eyelashes thawing. Maybe a little heat was leaking from one of the adjoining store fronts. It wasn't really warm enough to undo his coat, but at least he knew he wouldn't freeze.

On one end of the bench was a pile of newspapers, neatly folded. Logan lay down and spread the papers over his legs as best he could. Too dark to read any more of the notebook, he listened to the plastic blow around outside the window and tried to push thoughts of his rugby team out of his mind. What about driving? He could think about that. His mom had signed him up to start lessons in the spring, but he didn't need them. He knew how to drive, not that it really mattered. The chances of getting a car from his dad likely evaporated when he didn't make the team. No rugby scholarship. No beaming father. *Life sucks and then you die, Dad*, he thought. *Haven't you figured that out by now?*

He didn't want to think about his dad, shacked up with his new secretary-slash-girlfriend in Denver. His dad had probably heard all about Logan getting booted off the team by now.

Logan shivered a little and tucked his left arm under his head. He'd think about the lists of cars he had made for Abbie. Right. That was safer. He'd dig through her notebook and read them over again in the morning to see if he'd changed his mind at all. Maybe he needed to reconsider a few newer models. Maybe the Zephyr merited a place on the list after all — just because. And thinking of running boards and gull wings, Logan fell asleep with Abbie's notebook as his only pillow against the hard wood of the old bench.

10

It was like someone was touching his face, over and over again. Maybe butterfly wings or a feather tickling him. Butterfly feathers? Whatever it was, it was damn irritating. Logan reached up to brush it away and cold shot though him like ice water in his veins. He sat up, immediately awake, the pages of a newspaper pooling around his feet on the cement floor.

The butterfly wings had been snow. In the night the plastic had blown off the tiny window above the door and now the snow swirled in — the same big fat flakes filling the air outside. The sky through the glass was now white instead of black, so it must be daylight, though there was no sign of sun. It was cold enough in here for the snow to skiff across the floor — not melting. But under his makeshift blanket of newspapers it had been warm — or at least warm enough to offer Logan the peace of a few hours slumber, anyway.

He propped his elbows on his knees and tried to rub a bit of the sleep from his eyes. His mouth tasted like a dragon had slept in it. He grinned a little at the thought of what his dad would have to say if he knew Logan had slept on a wooden bench inside an abandoned storefront. He wasn't quite sure of the actual words, but he knew what the tone of voice would be. Loud. And his mother would want to raise money for a shelter for the disadvantaged. Or contribute to a food bank. She had a soft heart and the truth was he loved her for it. She was his mother, after all. But she had no damned sense. So busy solving other people's problems.

Logan's own problems came flooding back to him. He needed to talk to Kip in case Cleo had contacted him. And he needed to get something warm inside him, because the river of ice in his veins was making him sleepy again. And that kind of sleepy in this kind of cold was not a good thing.

Shadows moved in among the snowflakes swirling out on the street and Logan thought a cup of tea from The Bean and Gone might be just the thing while he used their internet connection. His body creaked as he stood up, so he stretched and then paused a moment to collect the newspapers into a pile, leaving them neatly on the bench. Someone else might need them — someone who probably didn't have the price of a cup of tea to warm themselves after a cold night. He pulled his hat down low and yanked up his hood as he slid sideways through the broken board. He had to quit thinking like that; he was starting to sound like his mother.

*　　*　　*

The Bean and Gone was bustling as commuters stopped for coffee on their way to work. In Clearwater, the snow might fly and the slush might pile but life still muddled on.

It had taken him a while to figure out, but now it seemed so obvious where she was headed. And he was sure that as soon as her family found out she was missing, they would figure it out, too. But who knows? Maybe her family were as out of touch as Cleo said they were. In her mind there was only one person who knew her and loved her for herself. And maybe now she needed her Nona more than ever before. But Nona was pretty sick. And time was short.

Logan sat down at an internet station and tucked his tea carefully into the cup-holder off to one side. He was the only customer using a computer — two others sat idle. He clicked onto the internet and focussed on the screen.

No new mail. Freakin' Tom. Logan counted messages in his sent file. Three unanswered messages. Some great friend and supporter Tom turned out to be. And nice of the coach to keep in touch, too. Logan sighed and leaned his head onto his hand for a moment. Sometimes it just felt like too much to deal with. Everything had changed. Nothing was safe or easy anymore. But Cleo wasn't safe right now either. He sat up and pushed the feelings away for another time. He'd deal with all the crap in his life later. Right now he had a job to do.

Time to Google. He flipped open the back of Abbie's

notebook. Inside the back cover, she had basic information logged in neat rows. Names, phone numbers, e-mail, family names, next of kin.

He ran his finger down the column to Cleo's name.

Name: Cleopatra Jones. Nickname: Jacqueline. (Abbie had put a little smiley face beside the word. She obviously thought it was cuter than he did.) Special people: Mother — Donna-Fay; Grandmother — (Nona) Sophia Jones.

Okay, he knew her name already from Cleo's essay. What about an address or a phone number?

But there was nothing. Still, how many Sophia Joneses could there be in a tiny place like this? He could probably look her up in the phone book in seconds.

Logan flipped screens to log into his instant message account. He hit the enter button and immediately there was a message.

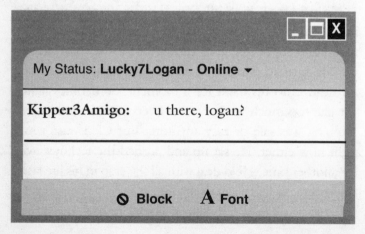

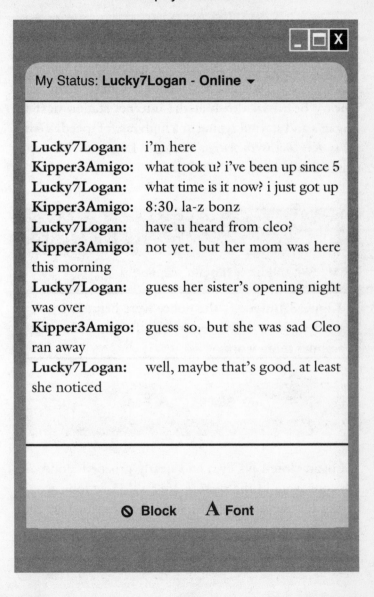

There was a pause while Kip typed his reply. Logan sipped his tea and took a bite of the banana bread he'd bought for breakfast. The kid was a slow typist with too much to say. Deadly combination. A burly man with a heavy beard sat down at the internet station next to Logan's and started typing at a high rate of speed. *That's what Kip needs to learn,* thought Logan as his reply chime finally rang.

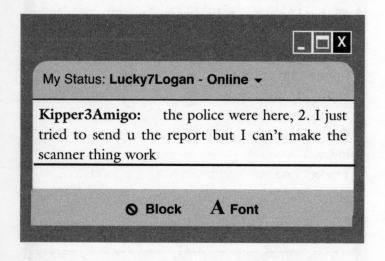

My Status: **Lucky7Logan - Online** ▾

Kipper3Amigo: the police were here, 2. I just tried to send u the report but I can't make the scanner thing work

🚫 **Block**   **A Font**

Logan closed his eyes and nearly groaned aloud. So the cops were in the picture after all. How long would it take for them to call the local detachment here and grab Cleo? But he was here and they weren't — the advantage might not be all theirs just yet. He typed a reply as quickly as he could.

My Status: **Lucky7Logan - Online** ▾

Lucky7Logan: kip, what did the police have to say? did they ask u any questions?

Kipper3Amigo: they said it was really common for kids with eating disorders to run away but that they would wait for 24 hours to see if she would come home. since it's so cold outside they figured they could find her quick because there aren't so many places 2 hide. they asked me if she told me where she was going

Lucky7Logan: did u tell????

Kipper3Amigo: NO!!!!! I wouldn't tell on Cleo. wait a sec

Lucky7Logan: what's happening?

Kipper3Amigo: i just checked e-mail to see if she'd sent 1. not yet

🚫 **Block**   **A** **Font**

My Status: **Lucky7Logan - Online** ▾

Lucky7Logan: r u sure she's going to contact u?
Kipper3Amigo: she promised. she wouldn't say where she was going but she promised she would let me know she was safe
Lucky7Logan: ok, well I have to sit here for a minute and look something up. i'll stay on line just in case for a few more minutes
Kipper3Amigo: gr8. and thanks for doing this, Logan. i'm really scared for Cleo
Lucky7Logan: don't be scared. she's tough. and I'm going to find her, anyway

🚫 **Block**   A **Font**

Logan flipped open his e-mail again. Still nothing. He clicked the "create message" button.

To: tommykixa$$@coldlist.com
From: rugbyrox@yowza.com
———————————————————————

Hey, Tom. Howareya? Maybe you heard I missed the tryouts. Coach called me to say I'm off the team. Guess there's always next year ...

His stomach suddenly sour, he leaned back in his seat to toss the rest of his banana bread in the garbage. What was the use? There wasn't really any more to say. He had to roll his chair forward a little as someone pushed by to get to the last open internet terminal. Logan stared glumly at the screen for a minute and then reached over and punched the delete key. Tom and the rest of the team had moved on. And next year? What a joke. Dr. Jekyll and Mr. Crohn had landed in his gut and had no plans to leave anytime soon. He'd be lucky if he even made team waterboy.

The chime sounded again.

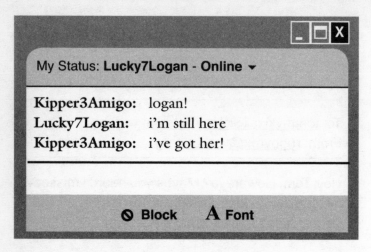

Kipper3Amigo: logan!
Lucky7Logan: i'm still here
Kipper3Amigo: i've got her!

Logan leaned forward in his chair.

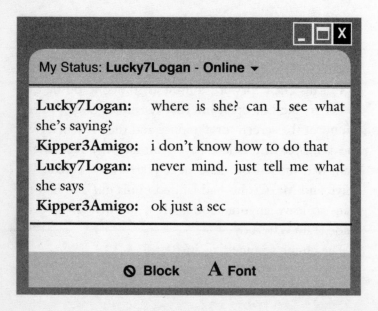

Lucky7Logan: where is she? can I see what she's saying?
Kipper3Amigo: i don't know how to do that
Lucky7Logan: never mind. just tell me what she says
Kipper3Amigo: ok just a sec

Logan leaned back and took a sip of tea. It was tepid, but he hardly noticed. His heart was pounding and he actually felt a little sweaty in his heavy coat. He took a minute to hang it over the back of his chair and pulled Abbie's notebook, rolled up in its plastic bag, from the large outside pocket. The sounds of people chatting, ruffling newspapers and the pinging of the other computers washed over him. He thought about buying something from the little retail section of the store for Kip. He was a good kid; maybe something from Clearwater would cheer him up — a souvenir of his help in finding Cleo. If he ever found her.

The chime pinged.

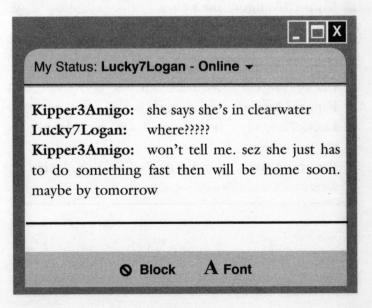

My Status: **Lucky7Logan - Online** ▾

Kipper3Amigo: she says she's in clearwater
Lucky7Logan: where?????
Kipper3Amigo: won't tell me. sez she just has to do something fast then will be home soon. maybe by tomorrow

🚫 **Block**   **A** **Font**

Great, Logan thought. *I go on this big rescue mission and the damsel isn't even in distress. But hey — I did get to be in a near bus-crash and sleep all night on a freezing wooden bench.* But his stomach seemed to unclench just a little. *At least she's not going to do anything crazy.* He leaned forward but Kip's icon flashed again. One of the internet users brushed by him on their way out.

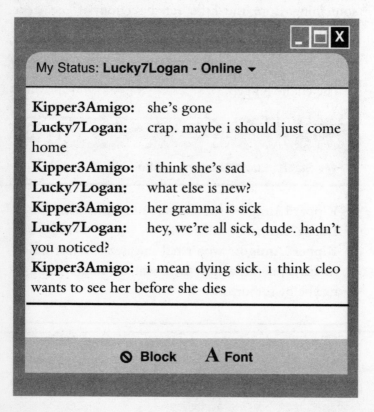

My Status: **Lucky7Logan - Online** ▾

Kipper3Amigo: she's gone
Lucky7Logan: crap. maybe i should just come home
Kipper3Amigo: i think she's sad
Lucky7Logan: what else is new?
Kipper3Amigo: her gramma is sick
Lucky7Logan: hey, we're all sick, dude. hadn't you noticed?
Kipper3Amigo: i mean dying sick. i think cleo wants to see her before she dies

🚫 **Block** **A** **Font**

For the first time in hours, Logan remembered the contents of his inner coat pocket. He leaned back and shrugged into his coat, and dropped his tea cup into the bin.

My Status: Lucky7Logan - Online ▾

Kipper3Amigo: u still there logan?
Lucky7Logan: yep
Kipper3Amigo: u coming home?
Lucky7Logan: yeah. but i've gotta do something first. hey kid?
Kipper3Amigo: yeah?
Lucky7Logan: thanks for the help. u rule
Kipper3Amigo: thanx logan!!!!!

🚫 **Block**   **A Font**

If Logan had typed another word he would have missed the flash of red. But he'd logged off and stood up to pull money out of his pocket to pay for the internet time. And that's when he saw it: a giant red sweater on the back of a tiny female who was running out the door. He knew both the sweater and the person inside it instantly.

Crap. He looked over at the other internet stations. The burly guy in the big coat was just getting to his feet. The other one was empty. She'd been typing practically right beside him and he hadn't even noticed.

He dropped a ten-dollar bill on the counter and roared out the door after her. He was only five feet out of the store when he remembered he'd left Abbie's notebook at the internet station and ran back.

"You want your change, sir?" the attendant called.

"Keep it," he puffed, grabbing the notebook and plastic bag and bolting for the door again. He ran down the street in the direction she'd headed, but she was gone. *That's the way these things happen,* he thought. *You nearly get what you want and then it just slips away.*

Logan leaned against a lamppost to force himself to actually stop and think a moment. He didn't have to chase her. He knew where she was going. And how many old-age homes could there be in Clearwater? The town had a population of less than three thousand people. How many of them would have little old ladies named Sophia? It should only take a minute to figure it out. *Just use a little logic, Logan,* he thought. *When Plan B evaporates in your face, go back to Plan A.*

He turned on his heel and headed back to the

coffee shop. The attendant beamed at him and handed the local telephone directory over as soon as he asked for it.

He sat down with the yellow pages and looked up Old Folks. Nothing. A chill came over him. What if she was in someone's private home? What if she was dying in her own house? He looked up Sophia Jones. Nothing. S. Jones. Nothing. In desperation, he even looked up Nona Jones. That time he knew there'd be nothing. Where was she, anyway?

Dead end. He slumped back in his chair. *Abbie wouldn't let you quit like this,* he thought. *She'd want you to figure it out.*

He rubbed his eyes. *I can do this. Cleo might not know she needs me — but I've come this far. I've got to try.*

He waved at the attendant and logged back on to the nearest computer.

Something would happen to help him. He looked to the sky for a bolt of lightning, but the ceiling of The Bean and Gone just looked ordinary. A little brown water stain in one corner — that was all. He turned his attention to the screen. It had defaulted to some local homepage for Clearwater. No help there.

He was just about to log off the computer when a pop-up ad emerged.

Sheesh. He picked up the yellow pages and flipped through until he found Retirement Communities and Homes. Okay, so they weren't listed as old folks' homes after all. And he was Logan, King of the Idiots.

There were three listed. He tore out the page, threw the directory at the startled attendant, and ran out the door.

*   *   *

Logan's Rule of Three: if you have three places to look, you'll look in the wrong two first. But his luck must have been changing — he hit it on the second try. The first place, Sunrise Manor, had been an immediate washout. Sunrise Manor — who named these places, anyhow? And who did they think they were kidding? Maybe

Sun*set* Manor had been taken. A quick conversation with the clerk at the front desk only confirmed that a Mrs. Jones did not reside there.

But ...

"Mrs. Sophia Jones?" the clerk asked.

Logan took a quick peek at Cleo's essay in the notebook. He didn't want to make another stupid mistake. "Yeah — that's her."

"Oh, I know Mrs. Jones. She's one of my neighbours, just down Front Street."

Thank God for small town nosiness, thought Logan.

"She's resting at Shady Pines. It's over on the other side of town, on Logan."

Logan nodded and stuffed the notebook back in the bag, before turning back to the clerk. "What street did you say?"

The clerk nodded, patience clearly one of her strong suits. "Logan Street, young man. Shady Pines is on Logan. You just follow Front Street round to the other side of the lake and you can't miss it. Are you one of her relatives? A grandson, perhaps?"

"Uh ... no. Not a grandson. I'm ... uh ... friends with her granddaughter. Thanks for your help." He stumbled out the door. Nona was resting on Logan Street. Logan Street!

He doubted Nona was doing much resting. She seemed more like the fighter type. But you couldn't beat the address.

He poked his head back in the door. "Is there a bus to get there? It's pretty cold outside."

The clerk smiled and walked around the front of the desk. "Well young man, I'm heading home for a cup of tea right now. Let me give you a lift."

And, in the end, it was easy as that.

11

This time he wasn't taking any chances. He gave a cheery wave to the nice desk clerk as she drove off. *Too bad she's stuck with a lousy Isuzu,* he thought. *Crappy vehicle.* By the time he walked into Shady Pines he'd decided that they would be more likely to let him in if he became Cleo's long lost cousin.

"Oh ... I thought the family were not able to arrive until tomorrow," the newest front desk clerk said, checking her notes after he'd made his request. Her name tag gleamed under the fluorescent lights: Mrs. Beadle.

"That would be her daughter," Logan said, with a smile. "But I was in town today so I thought I'd take the opportunity ..."

Mrs. Beadle nodded, her head at a sorrowful tilt. "It's well you have come today," she said quietly, and he was surprised to see her eyes fill with tears. Maybe this was more than just a job after all.

"The whole town knows Mrs. Jones," she said as she led Logan down the hall. "We will all miss her terribly. She's a wonderful woman."

Mrs. Beadle stopped at the last door in the hall, her hand on the knob. "Don't be alarmed if a nurse pops her head in," she said. "We've been checking every half hour or so. It won't be long now, I'm afraid."

She swung open the door and gave a little gasp of shock. Cleo was sitting, her head bowed at the side of the bed, holding her Nona's hand.

"Why ... who are you?" asked Mrs. Beadle, clearly startled.

"She's my cousin. Sophia's granddaughter," blurted Logan, praying Cleo would play along.

But when she spoke, Cleo's voice was filled with an indescribable sadness. "I'm Cleo Jones. I just slipped in the back door," she said quietly. "This is ... was ... my Nona."

"Oh my dear," said Mrs. Beadle. "Let me call the nurse."

But Cleo shook her head, her eyes on Logan. She stood up and placed Nona's hand gently on the bedspread.

"I think maybe we'd like a moment alone with Nona," said Logan, his voice cracking only a little. He felt a bit dizzy but was not about to admit it to anyone.

Mrs. Beadle nodded immediately. "Please take all the time you need. We have everything set as soon as you are ready."

She patted Logan gently on the back and quietly withdrew, closing the door behind her.

"How did you find me?" asked Cleo, sitting back down in the chair beside the bed.

Logan couldn't tear his eyes away from Sophia. This was the first dead person he had ever shared a room with and she most definitely did not look like she was sleeping. He tried to pull himself together for Cleo's sake.

"I just figured you'd need to see your grandmother since she was ... uh ...," he said. His mouth felt strangely dry. He tried again. "And this is a small town. Everyone knows her. She wasn't hard to find."

"Logan, you don't look so well," Cleo said. She stood up and turned towards him just in time to bear the full weight of the former rugby player as he fell into her arms.

*   *   *

"You sure you're all right young man?" Mrs. Beadle gave a final wipe to Logan's forehead with a damp towel.

He nodded, more embarrassed than he could ever remember being in his life. "I'm fine, really. It's just been a long couple of days and I didn't sleep very well last night," he said.

"Thank you for all your help, Mrs. Beadle," said Cleo, her voice muffled by the wad of cloth she still held to her own face. "We'll be fine now." The clerk smiled again, but left the door open this time. "Just call if you need me," she said.

"Please tell me I haven't broken your nose," said Logan, eyeing the bloody rag in Cleo's hand.

"It's pretty sore, but I don't think it's actually broken," she said, examining the rag critically. "Lots of blood, though." She raised a sarcastic eyebrow at him. "I can't tell you how happy I am that you've come to help out."

"Yeah, well, sorry about that," he said.

"I'm just kidding, Logan, you know that. I can't really think of anyone I'd rather have here right now."

They sat together quietly for a moment. "Did you get a chance to talk with her at all?" he asked at last

"A bit, I guess," said Cleo, setting the cloth aside. The blood flow had finally stopped. "But she wasn't herself, really. I think she was mostly gone, to tell you the truth. She wasn't coherent — not the way she always used to be."

Cleo looked at him and for the first time her eyes showed the traces of tears. "I wanted to tell her about everything that has happened and to confess about losing the astrolabe. But she left me before I could even apologize."

The astrolabe. Logan opened his mouth to speak, but just then Mrs. Beadle put her head through the door and looked from Logan to Cleo and back again. "The funeral home director is here. Would you like to speak with him now?"

Cleo shook her head. "Perhaps a little later," she said. "I need to talk a little with my ... my cousin first."

"Whatever you'd like, dear," said Mrs. Beadle. Cleo

nodded at the clerk as she left the room and turned away from the bed.

"Let's go home," she said, and she took Logan firmly by the hand.

"Home?"

"Nona's place, of course."

Cleo smiled a little and gestured to the body of her grandmother. "That's not her anymore. She's gone — and I want to see her place before she's gone from there, too." She picked up her own coat and stuffed Logan's things into his hands.

Logan felt puzzled, but keeping his eyes carefully averted from the bed, he followed Cleo out the back door. "No need to run into the staff again," she said by way of explanation, "and it's a shorter walk this way." She pulled her hat right down to her eyes and pushed her hands into red mittens as she started off down the street. Logan shrugged into his coat and followed her, jogging a little to catch up.

The snow had stopped and the air was quiet. A single set of tire tracks marked the way along the silent road where they walked.

It took a moment before Logan noticed the small black bag dangling from Cleo's wrist.

"It's Nona's purse," she said when he asked. "It was the only thing she was clear about when she spoke to me. She made me take it, so I hid it in the sleeve of my sweater so the staff wouldn't think I was stealing from my dead grandmother."

Logan was feeling a momentary rush of admiration for Cleo's felonious behaviour when he nearly tripped over her. She had stopped suddenly in the middle of the sidewalk and he realized she was crying. Full out — not just leaking a little around the eyes. In seconds it progressed to heavy sobs, tears pouring down her face, hiccupping breath — the whole package. A moment after that her legs started to wobble so much he feared she might fall onto the frozen ground.

He put an arm around her to steady her and looked desperately about for somewhere to take her. They were only a few strides from a bus shelter, so he pulled her inside and helped her down onto the bench before she could fall.

He didn't know what else to do, so he took one of her red mittens in his hands and waited.

She leaned against his shoulder and cried.

The snow had almost stopped and the cold had lost some of its sharpness — somehow muted a little. The girl beside him cried on. Logan just sat there and looked out at the day.

A bus pulled up, but he waved it away. The bus driver gave him a cheery wave back.

Cleo kept crying.

Logan wondered how long one person could continue to produce tears at this rate. He'd never seen anything like it.

After what felt like hours, she started to hiccup. He passed her a crumpled napkin covered in banana bread crumbs to clean her face. It was all he had in his pocket.

"Thank you," she said, and blew her nose. "I'm sorry. I don't know why that happened. I guess I've just never thought of Nona as my dead grandmother before."

Logan nodded. He wasn't sure that there was anything he could safely say, so for once he kept his mouth closed.

It was the right thing to do.

Ten minutes later, Cleo led them up the front walk of a neat bungalow on Front Street. Only a thin skim of snow lined the walk.

"The neighbours keep the sidewalks clear," Cleo said. She opened Nona's purse and drew out the house key, attached to a little chain with a house dangling from it.

"Are you really okay?" Logan asked as she opened the front door. He was feeling a little worried about the possibility of another crying jag.

"Yeah. I'm fine," she said. And in they walked.

*   *   *

"Wouldja look at this place? It's like some kind of museum."

Logan saw Cleo smile a little at that, though her eyes and nose were still bright red. It was good to see some colour in her face, if only from crying.

kc dyer

"I told you she was special," she said, running her fingers through a thin film of dust on the tabletop. "Didn't you read my essay?"

"Oh, yeah, sure. I just forgot, that's all."

"You totally did not read it. Too bad. It was an amazing piece of writing. Abbie gave me an A. It's probably still there, in your stolen goods." She pointed to Abbie's notebook, the one corner of the cover that stuck out from the plastic looking considerably worse for its journey.

"Look, I only stole Abbie's notebook so I could use it to find you. Maybe I didn't have time to read the whole thing."

For the first time, she peered at him closely. "You're lying," she said after a moment. "I think you really did read it after all. You're only saying you didn't read it because you think cool guys don't read."

"Not true."

"It is so. And that's where you're wrong, bucko. Cool guys do read. And write, too. Look at Holden Caulfield."

"Holden Caulfield was a figment of J.D. Salinger's imagination," Logan snapped. "He wasn't a real person."

"Ha!" Cleo's face registered something other than pain for the first time that day. "I knew you'd get that. Means you had to have read the book, moron."

Logan rolled his eyes. There was no arguing with the female of the species. She was like a dog with a bone in its teeth — might as well just give up now. "Yeah, well,

182

I only read that because Abbie told me I might like it. That and a book of poetry by Robert Frost. *And* she took away my Xbox, so I had nothing better to do."

"Anyway," Cleo continued, still smug from her small victory. "Since you read my essay, you should remember that Nona collected antiques."

Logan looked around again. "My grandmother collects antiques, too," he admitted, "but this house looks nothing like hers. Her house is huge and old and filled with pieces of smelly furniture, and each one weighs seven tons."

Cleo shook her head. "Nona may have been an astronomer, but she was all about fun. She only collected old things that she thought were extremely cool." She reached down and picked up a strange looking instrument from a side table. "This sextant, for example. Nona told me she found it in the garbage at one of the observatories she worked in. Guess somebody thought that new technology was better, but Nona liked it, so she kept it."

A thought suddenly struck Logan and he leapt to his feet. He returned from the front hall with the contents of his inner jacket pocket.

"Here's something you might want back," he said, ducking his head a little as he handed her the astrolabe. "I meant to give it back earlier, but —"

"Logan!" she said, clearly ecstatic. "Where did you find it?"

He was tempted to make something up — like maybe he'd found it under her bed in the hospital room — but in the end, he just told the truth. "You threw it at me the night I got mad at you for hiding the laxative wrappers in my recycling," he said.

She laughed a little. "Author of my own misfortune, I guess. I was past rational thinking at that point — just throwing anything to get you to stop talking. To stop reminding me of the things I do wrong."

"But I ..."

"I know. You were just saying what you thought was right. And it *was* right. But I was so sick of always being handled, Logan. Blood pressure cuff. Temperature. Heart rate monitor. Gastric tube. Intravenous drip. You must know what I mean, you've been there, too. I just wanted them to leave me alone. When the feeding tube came out I thought I would be free of them for at least part of the time. But Medusa was measuring my food output. Do you know what that means?"

Logan was silent a moment, watching Cleo running her fingers over the small metal astrolabe. "I guess it means you thought she deserved to find a little dog shit in the toilet."

Cleo grinned. "Exactly."

12

A candle flickered from inside a jam jar and reflected off the polished surface of the old dining table.

"Nona would have liked this," Cleo said. "She loved spontaneity."

Logan looked across at her and grinned. "What would she have thought about the menu?"

The table was not exactly groaning under the weight of a feast. A quick search through Nona's pantry yielded little that either of them was either interested in or able to eat. So, they drank tea, ate toast, and Cleo splurged on a spoonful of peanut butter.

"I've given up barfing," she said conversationally.

Logan grinned, not put off in the least from his dinner. "How do you know?" he asked. "Maybe as soon as you get back around the skinny chick at school or your sister you'll want to start again."

"No," she said firmly, chewing her toast. "I decided last night. After the cab let me off at the rest home, I hiked over and hid in the bathroom of the community centre. Sitting with my feet up on the toilet until they shut off the lights gave me a chance to think."

"Good place for thinking, toilets," Logan said.

"Not for me. I usually spend my time in the washroom trying *not* to think about what I am doing." She took a sip of tea. "Anyway, I really do want to try to have more fun in my life. Not like Adine and her rainbow-party kind of fun. I want to be more like Nona — the one I remember, not the one I saw today. I need to get rid of some of the crappy stuff from my past. Including throwing up every time I eat."

Logan was silent a moment, thinking. "I still don't really get it, you know."

"Get what? The barfing?"

"Yeah — well, that and everything else. I mean, look at you; you are a beautiful girl. Or you would be if you had a little meat on your bones." He ignored Cleo's glare and stumbled on, determined to finish what he'd set out to say. "It's just been really hard for me, y'know. Watching you starve yourself — for the sake of what? Did it make you smarter or better than anyone else? Did it make you happier?"

Cleo dropped her eyes.

"No, it didn't make me happier. It just sort of took hold of me. I couldn't think of anything else. It was like, if I controlled the food, it meant I would look great and everything else would be all right."

"Uh, I hate to break it to you, but you don't look great with your bones sticking through your skin."

She glared at him across the table. "Okay, I just said I'd given up being sick. I've figured it out, all right?"

Logan reached across the table and touched her arm. Cleo stiffened, but finally let him take her hand in his.

"I don't think you have got it all figured out," he said quietly. "But the reason I came to find you was to let you know that if you need a little support along the way, I'm here."

Cleo looked at him a long time, her eyes large in the candlelight. Logan steeled himself for the usual verbal onslaught when she finally opened her mouth, but instead of the whole chain of excuses he expected to hear, all she said was "Thanks."

*   *   *

Logan woke as the first light of dawn crept through Nona's lace curtains. He pulled himself up off the couch, grateful for its comfort after the bench of the night before. They'd sat for hours after dinner, just talking and looking out the window at the stars. Cleo had shown him how to use the astrolabe and the sextant. He'd told her about his decision to try for a job as volunteer coach for the rugby squad at the middle school next year. They had both expected the police or her parents to show up — but nothing. Not even a phone call. He didn't remember falling asleep, but this morning, somehow he felt completely rested for the first time in months.

He could hear Cleo in the kitchen, knocking dishes

together and splashing. He rubbed the sleep out of his eyes.

"Logan!"

Cleo's voice was muffled from the distance, but there was no mistaking her urgency. Logan jumped up, instantly alert, and ran through the doorway. "What is it?"

He found her standing in the pristine kitchen, all blue and white cheerfulness in the morning light. Cleo stood beside the countertop, a strange look on her face. On the counter was Abbie's notebook, open to the last page. And in her hand was a small, white envelope.

"What is it?" Logan repeated, striding over to stand beside her.

"I must have missed it in the dark last night," she said. "I think it's a note — to me."

"Uh, did you pick that up from the fact that it has 'CLEO' written on it in huge letters?"

"Okay, Mr. Smarty-pants. It's just ... she said yesterday she'd left me something, remember? When I was talking to her in the nursing home."

"Cleo, by the time I got there, you were holding hands with an ex-grandmother."

She glared at him and turned the envelope over in her hands.

"Words from the dead. That's a bit creepy, isn't it?" he muttered.

"Thank you, Mister Sensitivity," she said flatly.

"Maybe I should just read it."

"Good idea."

She opened the small envelope and pulled out a heavily folded piece of paper. As she undid the first fold, a silver key fell out and clattered onto the countertop. It was attached to a thin chain with a tiny car on it. Logan slapped his hand on the key to stop it sliding to the floor.

"What's that?"

"It's a key, goofball."

"I can see that," he replied impatiently. "My question is, what is it a key to?" He looked at the keychain. "A car, maybe?"

"Nona hasn't driven since I've known her, so your guess is as good as mine." Cleo unfolded the rest of the letter, a surprisingly large piece of paper with both sides closely covered in a spidery script.

Logan took one look at the length of the letter and turned away to prowl the cupboards. It was time for breakfast.

The phone on the counter rang with a shrillness that made them both jump.

"Are you going to answer that?" he asked after the second ring.

"I don't want them to know I'm here," Cleo said. "Unless ..."

The answering machine attached to the phone clicked on and a lively voice spoke.

"This is Sophia. You've missed me. Leave a message."

Cleo's face was white. "Nona …," she whispered.

"Cleopatra darling, are you there? It's Mother. If you are there, please pick up the phone."

Logan reached for the receiver but Cleo pushed his hand away, gesturing wildly. Her mother's voice continued.

"Sweetie, I've just come off the phone with Mrs. Beadle at the nursing home. They told me you were with Nona when she passed yesterday. I'm … I'm a little confused, sweetie-pie. I got a message from the hospital on my voicemail saying you'd been transferred to a different unit, but when I called the hospital, they said you'd been signed out for a weekend pass. But never mind that now — we can sort it all out later. Honey? Are you there? Please pick up. I'm so sorry, baby, I wanted to spare you this after all you've been through lately."

"You should talk to her, Cleo," said Logan. "Hurry, before she hangs up." He reached for the phone again, but his hand froze at her next words

"Honey, I'm coming down to get you. Logan's dad is here, too. I know he's with you down there. Mrs. Beadle said you were there with someone claiming to be your cousin …"

"Oh, now that's good," muttered Cleo. "They probably think we planned all this."

"Shhh!" said Logan, trying to hear.

"... all have a lot to talk about, don't you think? We'll be there ..."

Click.

The answering machine cut her off and the tape began to rewind.

"Oh, great," said Logan. "Some kind of freakin' modern answering machine your Nona has — now we don't even know when they are going to get here."

Cleo still looked like she'd seen — or heard — a ghost.

"I think maybe you need a cup of tea," he said quietly, mentally kicking himself. She was right — he really was Mr. Sensitivity. Not.

Cleo spoke through white lips. "We need to decide what to do, don't you think? She said your dad ..."

"Just think a minute. It's okay. Even if they leave right now, it'll still take them a couple of hours to get here," Logan said. "Let me get you a drink at least." Cleo nodded and turned back to the letter.

Logan walked into the pantry but found himself staring blindly at the shelves. *Dad? Here? Why would ...?*

His thoughts were interrupted by the distant sound of a slamming door. His heart went into his throat. How could they be here already?

Logan stuck his head into the kitchen. "Is somebody ..."

But the kitchen was empty.

Hunger forgotten, Logan grabbed his coat and ran for the door. He leaped over a broom Cleo had left tilted against the wall but caught the toe of his shoe and crashed heavily to the floor. By the time he wrenched open the front door there was no sign of her. He stared stupidly down at the footprints still frozen on the doorstep from the night before. No fresh prints, so he slammed the door shut and headed for the back of the house. He hadn't been back here before and it took a minute to find the door. It wasn't quite closed and a pall of cold hung in the air. But when he opened it he could see where she'd bolted through the large yard and past an outbuilding.

Logan ran back inside to grab his shoes and saw the letter where she'd dropped it on the floor. His heart still hammering, he walked over and picked up the letter. What was going on in that girl's head? Maybe the letter held the answer.

The key was still on the counter. His fingers toyed with it absently as he read.

July 15

My darling Cleopatra,

I'm very tired these days, my dear and you mustn't fret about my imminent departure. I'm not one to hang around after a party gets dull. But the old girl has a few surprises left in her. Your mother will be able to stop worrying about pushing poor Helena toward a career as a terminal starlet. In your case, of course, your brains will carry you wherever you need to go, my dear. However, your Nona has made a few financial provisions for you as well. Somehow I don't think you care about money as much as your parents do and that is as it should be. Parents are made for worrying; it's what we do.

The worst thing about being gone will be missing out on watching the fun you are going to have in your life. But perhaps I won't miss it, after all. I may just hang around on some spiritual level to make sure you keep enough starch in your petticoats. (Just a little joke, my dear. Personally, I've never favoured petticoats.)

When I think of all the good times I've had in my life, I realize that most of them have stemmed from not standing still. I love to have roots; my home has been here in Clearwater since before your father was born. It is very important to me. But I must say I enjoyed my home the most when I was returning to it from someplace far away.

I don't think you've had exposure to nearly enough wandering, my dear. And I want to give you the opportunity. So let's just say this little silver object is more than just a key. It's a way of life. You will not be able to use it immediately, but as I know all too well, time passes more quickly than we ever imagine. I hope you embrace my gift to you and get as much enjoyment out of it as I have. I might add that over the years I found it never hurts to have a handsome navigator along for the ride.

Time for me to say a final goodbye now, Cleopatra. But, my girl, please remember this: when I say I will love you into eternity, that is exactly what I plan to do.

Your grandmother,

Nona Sophia

Logan dropped the letter onto the counter. He still didn't have a clue what Cleo was up to. *But she had quite the cool grandmother*, he thought. He picked up the key and examined it curiously. He rubbed his thumb across the tiny logo on the key again, and lifted his eyes slowly from the key, out the kitchen window to the small building behind the house. He ran for his shoes.

*　　*　　*

The door wasn't even locked. The handle turned as smoothly as any well-oiled machine in his hand. And even though the key dangled from his fist, he still couldn't quite believe the sight before his eyes.

Number one on the list.

Number one.

The Ferrari. His dream car.

Okay — it wasn't a 1961 — if he guessed right it was a '68 or a '69. And it wasn't silver. It was red.

Cherry red. A cherry red rag top. Logan leaned against the wall. After everything that had happened in the past few days, he wasn't completely sure he could trust his legs to hold him up.

He'd never been in the presence of a car like this one before. He'd never even known anyone who had been. His dad had talked about seeing one once, but even that was only at a distance.

It was beautiful. It was a jewel. But instead of dropping it into his lap, the car gods had bequeathed it to a weird skinny girl who couldn't even drive yet.

He ran his hand along the chrome and something akin to an electric shock shot through him, snapping him back to reality. He'd forgotten Cleo. Some helpful guy he was. The ex-rugby player drops the ball again. Where had she gone, anyway?

He looked out the garage window and realized she'd run towards the water. Was she suicidal with the light of day and the loss of her grandmother? Was the thought of her mother's arrival enough to make her want to throw herself into the lake? And what had he done to help? Fainted on her and nearly broken her nose. Fallen asleep on the couch. Time to get his act together.

He wiped his hands on his coat and then reverently placed them on the hood of the car again. Stealing a car was okay if the owner gave you the key, wasn't it? She'd left him the key, hadn't she? That made it not stealing. Of course it did.

But the car would never start. Not in this cold. Not a chance.

Logan looked around. Heated garage, car plugged into a block heater. Maybe the car gods didn't completely hate him after all.

Afterwards, he couldn't even remember sliding in behind the wheel. The vehicle started like a dream and purred like a panther. It didn't matter that he'd never heard a panther purr. If a panther purred, this is what it would sound like, no question.

"I might just have to kiss that little weirdie sometime," he said out loud, and then laughed at the sound of his own voice. But first he needed to find her.

Logan jumped out of the sleek, red machine and lifted the garage door up on its hinges. He didn't give a thought to flipping up the convertible top. He just hopped in and roared down the block toward the lake. Almost right away he caught a glimpse of her sweater, like a drop of blood against the falling snow. She was loping slowly along the shore beside the black water.

At the sight of her so close to the ice, Logan actually forgot about the car. All the fears he'd had for her came rushing back into his throat, making it hard to breathe. He careened off the road and down a boat launch ramp, screeching to a stop only as the tires hit the edge of the ice.

She looked over her shoulder and started running. Logan didn't stop to think. He jumped over the door of the car and bolted after her. He saw her glance over her shoulder again. She couldn't run very fast and he was gaining on her, his legs windmilling like a cartoon character on the slippery surface of rock and ice. She finally skidded to a stop and without a second glance at him, flung something high over the line of ice and dark water.

"What are you doing?" he yelled, trying to grab her to slow himself down.

"What are *you* doing?" she yelled back as he slid by. She reached out for him but her red mittens slipped uselessly across the back of his coat as his momentum carried him past her. His feet scrabbling for purchase and, totally out of control, he slid on.

At least it's me and not Cleo, he thought. Gravity finally won the fight and he fell to his knees in the slush, within an arm's reach of where the ice grew black and wet and became lake again. Right beside him was Cleo's missile.

It was wrapped in plastic. The corner was torn, and Logan didn't need to look inside to see the familiar cover. He scooped it up and inched backwards while the ice crackled ominously beneath him. One knee back ... one hand ... the other knee. And somehow the ice held.

After what seemed forever he scrambled back onto the rocky shore up to where she waited, shoulders drooping.

"Great throw," he said, panting. "You should consider pitching as a career."

Cleo sat on the rocky beach, hugging her knees to her scarlet sweater. She shrugged as he handed her the package and absently brushed some of the slush off it with her sleeve, dropping it beside her on the ground with a sigh.

"Typical. I couldn't even do this right."

"You maybe want to tell me what this is all about?" He sat down beside her on the beach, still panting a little. It was a pebbly, uncomfortable surface that didn't lend itself to prolonged sitting, in his estimation. Nevertheless, he stretched out his legs. He gingerly tried to lift some of the wet fabric away from his skin but his jeans were glued to his knees. He gave up. "I don't get it, Cleo."

She pulled her woollen hat a little lower and didn't meet his eyes.

"It's just got so many awful things in it. Getting caught barfing. Putting dog poop in the toilets. All the stupid stuff I did. Every failure. Good marks mean nothing when you're vomiting your life away and somebody's documenting your every mistake."

She picked up a rock and threw it onto the icy surface of the lake where it skittered a remarkably long way before coming to a rest.

"When I left the hospital, I was going to see Nona. But on the way here I decided I would never go back. Nobody would miss me — my mom is busy with my sister and her acting and my dad has his work at the college. I didn't know exactly what I was going to do, just that I had to get away from all of it. Then you showed up and everything changed. But when I heard my mom's voice on the answering machine, I just panicked. I had to get rid of the evidence; this notebook is like proof of all my mistakes."

Logan had to smile.

"You know it's all on computer, don't you? Abbie has an electronic file of all this stuff and so does the hospital. Throwing Abbie's notebook into the lake changes nothing. No matter how far you run, your records follow you forever."

She looked at him, incredulous. "But why would Abbie keep this, then? I mean, I've seen her working on the computer, but I just thought she was surfing the internet or something."

Logan shrugged and rubbed absently at the rime of frost that was creeping across the wet parts of his black gloves. It was cold ... and getting colder. "She's old fashioned, maybe. Teachers love notebooks and journals. Who knows what makes them do the things they do? And who cares, anyway? I don't. There's loads of crap in there about me, too, you know. All the stuff I wrote about how rugby is my future and what a hotshot lawyer my dad is." He shook his head. "None of it's true. My dad hasn't got the time of day for me. It's all crap."

She punched him gently on the arm. "It isn't, you know. So maybe you don't become a rugby star. You

still get to make it a part of your life — you told me
so yourself. And my mom said your dad was with her.
Maybe he's actually come back here to make things right
between you."

"He's always been too busy to notice that things
aren't right, Cleo. Why would that change now?"
Logan grabbed at the stump of a broken tree and hauled
himself to his feet with a grimace.

She shrugged. "I don't know. But he's here, not in
Denver. That's got to count for something, even if it's
only a start." She tossed another rock away and sighed.
"I guess since they are the only parents we've got, we'd
better start figuring out how to deal with them." She
swiped a mitten across her nose. "I'm sorry you had to
run out on the ice like that. It was a stupid thing for
me to do."

Logan reached down to help her up.

"I was mostly worried about you," he said. "And I
promised myself I'd give Abbie her notebook back, so I
couldn't let it go into the lake without a fight. But the
reason I came here was to make sure you were all right,
and instead you're the one giving me advice."

Cleo scrambled to her feet and looked up at him,
surprised. "I guess it's kinda nice to think about
someone besides myself," she admitted.

He brushed a tendril of hair away from the corner of
her mouth and kissed her gently where the crease of her
lip curved into her cheek.

She put her mittened hand up to the place he had kissed her. "Where did that come from?" she said slowly.

"I'm not sure," he said, and grinned a little. "It just felt like the right thing to do under the circumstances."

She grinned back at him. "Your gut hurting?"

He shook his head. "Nope. Yours?"

She shrugged. "Not really. I'm pretty cold, though."

"What else is new? How many sweaters are you wearing today? Ten?"

"Hey, my record is only seven. But I'm not doing that anymore. Giving it up — just like the barfing. I'm only wearing two today. But right now I kinda wish it was more."

"Well," he said. "You might be cold, but I'm cold and wet."

"Yeah, well you might be cold and wet, but I'm cold and wet and ...," she looked straight at him this time, "... I'm maybe a little hungry."

He grinned. "That Nona. She must've had some pretty powerful things to say to you before she died."

Cleo shrugged. "She didn't say much, but just seeing her again made me think. I guess I haven't done any real thinking in a while." She walked along beside him, quiet apart from the snow squeaking under her boots. "I can't eat a lot yet, you know. Like, I'm not ready for hamburgers with the works just yet."

"That's okay. I can't really eat 'em either, anymore. Sure do miss those bacon burgers with mayo, though."

She turned to make a face at him and slid a little on the ice.

He took one of her red-mittened hands to steady her. "I know a good coffee place in town. Will you settle for tea and toast before we head back to Evergreen?"

Cleo nodded. "One condition," she said, and reached into his pocket for the key. "You drive."

Epilogue

To:RugbyRox@yowza.com;
    cleo_jones@coldlist.com
From: KipperKK@childsafe.com

Hi Logan and Cleo,

I'm using Abbie's laptop to send this e-mail. She says hi! My new kidney is so good, I get to go home this week, just in time to put up the Christmas tree. Keep your fingers crossed for me. Life is always full of surprises, right?

Abbie says you will be coaching rugby at my school next year, Logan. Cool. I don't know how to play, but I can be the best cheerleader ever. You'll see.

I like your new e-mail address, Cleo. It's easier to spell. Things are pretty boring here without you guys. There's this new little kid. Her name is Rachel and now that her tonsils are gone she's supposed to go home tomorrow. She keeps following me around and driving me crazy. If you guys have any ideas to help me I sure would appreciate hearing them.

Kip — the New Kidney Kid

Acknowledgements

My thanks, as always, go out to those members of my friends and family who variously tolerate and abet my endeavours, thus allowing me to indulge in the egregious pastime of lying for my living. This book would not have been possible without teachers Kate Coombs and Elizabeth Raikhy for sharing their experiences and giving form to Abbie Zephyr. Thanks also to Doctor Jenny Druker and Doctor Linda Horspool for sharing their expertise of all things medical; to Spencer Corlett for the straight goods on decent cars and to Michael Hiebert for celestial inspiration and feedback on all things Sagan. Finally, thanks to my editor Barry Jowett for taking in his stride the concept of a novel named for a character who never actually appears, and to designers Alison Carr and Erin Mallory for realizing the shape of my ideas into two-dimensional form. Any errors that have occurred in the course of manoeuvring this story from out of my brain onto the page are my own.

This book goes out to anyone who, at one time or another in their lives, finds themselves somewhere outside the range of normal. Who says normal is so desirable, anyway?

~kc